DONALD'S INFERNO

A Novel Political Satire

Marji Smith

Donald's Inferno
A Novel Political Satire

This work is a political satire. Names of famous public figures are their names. Names of ordinary citizens, places and incidents are either the product of the author's imagination or are used fictitiously.

Published by
Charlie Publications

Library of Congress Control Number: 2018904144
ISBN 978-0-9858224-6-0

Printed and bound in the United States of America

Dedicated to the Ones—the resisting 65% With hope for the 35% addicted to Spraytan Orange. Admitting it is the first step toward recovery.

Donald's Inferno

A Novel Political Satire

His office was on a street called Twine, a seedy part of town infamously known as Donald's Inferno. Except for artillery casings and a tough-looking pigeon standing on the sidewalk a half block away, the early morning streets were empty. Small riots in this precinct usually didn't start until ten a.m., pandemonium from noon to nine, anarchy and mayhem peaking around midnight. It was just after seven-thirty, too early for mob rule.

Jason Nickle parked his light blue Prius precisely where the investigator instructed, between two yellow lines in front of the Halyard Winch Building, a dark red-brick four-story that ran the length of the block. Portions of the roof were blown off here and there, several upper-floor windows shattered and boarded over. Jason leaned across the seat and looked up at a second story window directly overhead. The detective's name was boldly printed in thick black letters:

Dr. Phil Magnum, P.I.

The window was clean, anyway, shiny, washed. Point for the dick.

His appointment wasn't until eight o'clock, but he'd left home extra early. Driving anywhere was a pain in the ass now, ever since left turns became illegal. Jason drummed his fingers on the steering wheel and glanced nervously in the rearview mirror. What time did miscreants and thugs and carjackers usually get up? Noon, maybe one o'clock, depending on how late they were out feloning. The only person stupid enough to be conscious on Twine Street at this hour was someone having a nervous breakdown. Him. Jason Nickle. A cold sweat glistened on his upper lip.

He should have brought some kind of protection. But what? He was afraid of guns. Maybe some ball-buster tool like a lug wrench or pliers. Were any hardware stores open? Did he have time? He glanced at his watch: fifteen minutes and one dirty stairwell away from his appointment with Magnum. Jason breathed deeply and closed his eyes. He should have brought an air horn.

"Okay, Amy," he muttered. "Here I am. I hope you're happy. I'm doing this for you." He rubbed his forehead irritably. "Okay, sorry. Point for you."

Storefronts up and down the block were locked behind heavy metal security gates: Cubic Hair, Hock-o-Sell, Nine 2 Fo-Five gun swap, a Spraytan Orange salon, Toy n' Joy, gaudy parlors with red or purple beaded curtains—places he'd only seen in gritty movies. Somewhere behind an open window someone was playing a saxophone; soulful, haunting, forlorn, the sound echoing down the long, deserted corridor.

Several blocks away, Balmer Yard sprawled to infinity. Jason could see a freight train hauling cargo across the Salmon Bay Bridge. His life was a train wreck, one long, fucking carload of screw-ups and failed heroism. Jumping off the bridge would be redundant. Just his luck a train would hit him first.

A movement on the sidewalk caught his eye. The pigeon ambled closer to his car, watching him. The saxophone wailed to a horrifying crescendo, like in the movies, Jason thought, just before body parts are ripped to shreds by razor teeth or sharp, rotating chains. My god, he might not make it into the building alive! He bolted from the car and flung the door closed in one swift movement, beeping the lock as he vaulted toward the stairwell. The pigeon was gaining fast.

Jason burst inside the building and slammed the door shut, panting hard with fear. The bird stood outside, staring up at him. They glared at each other through the dirty glass.

Jason gave it the finger. "I'm not taking any shit off you, you got that?"

He wiped his sweaty hands on his Dockers and studied the cluster of battle-weary mail boxes. Most were marked with graffiti; three had taped-on names: Dr. Phil Magnum, 201; Bed and Beaver, 304;

Clyde the Psychic, 401. Obviously other people lived or worked in the large building. Obviously it was nobody's business who or where they were. Jason had heard of the last one, Clyde the Psychic. He predicted the end of the 20th century and enjoyed fifteen minutes of fame until Trump took the credit.

Jason climbed the narrow wooden stairwell, dimly lit by a naked, low-wattage bulb halfway up, breathing as shallowly as humanly possible. Someone on an upper floor was hammering, the vibrations jarring fine particles of dust from the stained plaster walls and ceilings. He hated musty old buildings. This one had obviously never been renovated. If people knew the disgusting stuff in common dust they'd stick HEPA filters up their noses.

Halfway up he stopped, staring hard. Was that a spider web on the next step, there in the corner? He knew he should have brought a flashlight. It was a dirty web, the kind a black widow builds. Ohmygod, there it was! Shiny black body, red hourglass!

His left arm began to ache. His breath was short; he could vomit, too—classic heart attack symptoms. Had he remembered aspirin? He quickly felt his pockets and patted the little tin box. Okay, good. He gripped the railing, stretched over the next step, hoisted himself up and over and clamored noisily up to the first floor.

4

The detective's name was neatly printed on a solid wood door on the left:

DR. PHIL MAGNUM
PSYCHE INVESTIGATOR
Hang-ups—Kick-Starts—Detox-
Brain Frisking—Debuggings—Muckraking

Brain frisking? What kind of guy was this? Trying to intimidate him before he opened the door? "Lots of luck, buddy," he muttered under his breath. "All the good stuff's in my subconscious." He reached for the doorknob.

"It's open," a male voice said. "Come on in."

A man sitting behind a polished antique oak desk folded the morning paper and stood up, smiling. He looked about fifty-five, a little younger than Jason's father before he died. (Jason had a sudden flashback of Joseph Nickle; the quivering mustache, the imperious brow, the piercing eyes— cold, hard, dangerous eyes, like black ice. Fortunately, the image faded quickly.)

Except for a black fedora on the back of his head, Phil Magnum didn't fit the private eye movie stereotype, an unethical character in a cheap suit who bent the law and broke people's legs for twenty bucks. He wore neat black slacks, a white dress shirt with the cuffs folded back, a red-striped tie with a loosened knot, no suspenders, no shoulder holster and pistol. He didn't look hard-bitten, smart-assy, jaded by life as only someone in his profession could look, especially in this part of town. He looked like an easy-going guy. He had short, dark curly hair mixed with gray, thoughtful green eyes with deep frown lines between his eyebrows, and a likable face, not handsome, but nice. Jason still felt threatened.

"Jason Nickle?" Magnum said. He smiled warmly and extended his hand. "Phil Magnum."

They shook hands. "Jason Nickle," Jason said. He stood a little taller. "My friends call me Rocko."

"Would you like me to call you Rocko?"

Jason shrugged. "Maybe later. We just met."

"Good to meet you, Jason. Have a seat."

Phil gestured toward a chair identical to his own; sleek black tufted leather with a curved back and seat. Jason sat down, his body melding perfectly into the supple curves. He rubbed his hands over the luxurious leather arms. He could sleep in this.

It was a small office with only the two chairs, a coat-rack holding a black suit jacket, kitchenette in one corner, wastebasket, a box fan, an oak filing cabinet and the desk; nothing on it but a retro black desk phone, a banker's lamp with a green glass shade, and the folded newspaper. No pens, pencils, writing tablets, computer, files, stacks of paper, nothing. There was no reception area, no bosomy secretary snapping gum. The place was a step back in time, a Bogie movie in vintage drab.

6

There were two other doors, both closed, one probably for the bathroom. A small assortment of framed certificates hung on one wall, a large oil painting of a shipyard on another. Jason had seen the print someplace else, several times. He couldn't remember where.

"Have trouble finding the place?" Phil asked.

"Not really. Kind of a mean pigeon outside."

"He's okay, he works for me. Would you like something to drink? I just made coffee."

"Sure, okay. Coffee's good."

"I learned something interesting not too long ago." Phil puttered at a counter in the corner, next to a small refrigerator and microwave. "Coffee beans aren't really beans, they're actually seeds. They're pits inside red fruits that look like cherries, so they call them *cherries*." He filled two green mugs. "Cream?"

"Is it real cream?"

"Yes."

"Sure, okay."

Jason pushed a straggle of light brown hair away from his face. It was a Leonardo/Titanic look that never worked even when he was a teenager, but he kept the style anyway, hoping either his face or his luck would improve. His nose was perhaps his most interesting feature, Roman, with a conspicuous dent, size 2, Medium, measured with a ruler, brim to tip, for a nose guard he wore when the sidewalks

7

were icy. His eyes were blueish, but noticeably lighter and brighter after a colon cleanse.

Jason did not kid himself about his appearance. He was monotonous. He wasn't a man's man or a woman's man either, for that matter, based on the frequency he was dumped. He would never be anything but a generic man. Generic Jason. He sipped his coffee and glanced toward the window. The pigeon was perched on the ledge, pretending to ignore him.

Phil set a plate of assorted doughnuts and a stack of napkins on the desk. "I think we pretty well covered everything on the phone," he said. "If you have any more questions, ask away." He sat down and leaned back, relaxed, anticipating the next question. It was usually the first thing clients wanted to go over again at this stage.

Jason cleared his throat. "Well, uh, I'm not totally clear about your fee. I know you explained it to me, but I was picking myself off the floor."

"Okay."

"You said it was two thousand dollars."

"Yes."

"For one day."

"One full day, from now until eight o'clock tomorrow morning. If you want to leave sooner than that, that's up to you, but my fee is not refundable. This can only work if you stay the full twenty-four hours."

"In this room?"

"Except for going downstairs for lunch and dinner, the entire time will be spent here."

"What about sleeping?"

"Do you like your chair?"

"Yeah, it's great. Did it cost two thousand dollars?"

"Almost. I'm glad you like it. It's also your bed—if you sleep—but you won't, not much anyway." Phil waited a moment, then smiled. "Your next question is, why is your fee so friggin' high?"

"I was thinking another word, but yeah."

"Okay Jason, look at it from this perspective. If you went to see a doctor you'd be charged somewhere in the ballpark of a hundred dollars. For maybe fifteen minutes of their time. That's four hundred dollars an hour, nine-thousand, six-hundred dollars for twenty-four hours. Right?" Jason agreed that was right. "My fee is nowhere near that sum. The going rate for psychologists here locally is about two hundred dollars an hour, but you have to go in once a week, every week, month after month, sometimes year after year."

"But insurance pays most of it. It's a benefit after screwing me over."

"That is true. What I'm trying to explain is that this is a time-value choice, Jason. My fee is about eighty-three dollars an hour. The difference between me and them is that I cut to the chase in one day. Today."

Phil pressed his lips together thoughtfully, tapping his fingers on the desk. "Here's another way to look at it, Jason. How many things do we Tweet and text and post and pin and blog about ourselves every day? Most of it's filler, just letting the world know we're here, but sometimes we need answers now. My position is, why do we take the really important stuff, the shit that's totally fucking up our lives, and put it on some mule-team wagon train and wait however long it's going to take to get wherever it's going—if it makes it there at all—hoping someday we're going to get a fix? You know where the mule team always heads, Jason?" He made finger quotes. "*Our Past.*" Plod and slog, wallow and trudge, yada yada yada. Do you like this building?"

Jason was startled. "It's okay."

"Really?"

"No."

"Why not?"

"It smells."

"Like what?"

"Mold. Dust. Old smoke. My Aunt Brisky."

"That's right. Old smells. Smells from the past. Ancient history." He shook his head. "We're not going back there and wallow, Jason. We're going to drop in, grab a drink, have a quick look-around, then get the hell out of there. For the next twenty-four hours, you will be my exclusive client. Except for going to the bathroom, you're not leaving my sight. Our time doesn't start until you pay me. My fee also buys you a total of three phone calls anytime, day or night, good for the rest of your life."

"What if I use them up and I remember a conspiracy we didn't cover? I know from my dreams I have at least ten in my subconscious. What if I need a few more hours?"

"I already answered that question, but you won't. None of my clients have ever cashed in their calls. None. By this time tomorrow morning, you won't recognize the man sitting across from me now."

"Is that from the brain frisking?"

"Partly."

"I might need debugging, too. Is that extra?"

"No."

His success rate must be true, Jason thought. Although he never advertised, never solicited clients, Dr. Phil Magnum was solidly booked three months ahead. He kept such a low profile many locals thought he was an urban legend, mysterious and "deliciously romantic" according to Amy, but probably a Seattle myth. Except the myth cashed his five-hundred-dollar check.

"What's with the detox?" he said. "On your door?"

"I treat Spraytan Orange addictions. Free service."

"Aren't you scared you'll get caught?"

"No. The Bananas are . . ." He paused and smirked. "Okay, you can groan but the pun is accurate. They're too yellow to come up here. They've got bigger problems than me out there."

"I didn't think Complicits could be treated."

"Not the regime, they're making too much money, but once in a while a Novo comes in. It's rough to watch, the remorse, but at least they can sleep again at night."

Jason thought a moment, staring at his hands, then looked at Phil. "How do you know you can debug me? We've only talked a couple times on the phone."

Phil would never tell Jason how much he already knew going in, or how he learned it. He knew neighbors heard Jason sobbing when Trump won the election. He knew he was thirty-four, that his father, Joseph, was a far-right member of BAZOOKA who died from a sudden heart attack, that they didn't get along, that Jason bought a hybrid car with the inheritance money.

He knew his relationship with his mother, Beverly, was polite, that she moved to Naples, Florida and drove a black Peugeot with vanity plates she bought with the inheritance money, that she was often seen circling Fifth Avenue South until she found a prominent place to park where it would be easily recognized by her prominent new friends.

He knew the name of Jason's latest girlfriend, Amy McFine; that they met in McFine's Bakery, a family-owned business in Pike Place Market, that they had been living together four months and neighbors heard them arguing the last three, but not loud enough to call the cops. He knew she had recently called him an 'impotent whiner' in a public place.

He knew Jason did not have a police record, but a stop-and-frisk incident had been reported. Four incidents of flipping the bird to Complicits had also been reported. He knew he had a bachelor's degree, had been fired from his position as a health and safety specialist, that he currently worked at a mattress outlet store earning slightly more than minimum wage plus commissions, that despite being hugely overqualified for the job he worked hard and was pleasant to the customers.

He knew that Jason did not use drugs, prescribed or otherwise, ordered Manny's Pale Ale in sports bars and frequently bought corn dogs from a vendor near Freeway Park. He knew that Jason had never applied for a gun permit but did own a pair of Nikon 8 x 42 binoculars which he was often seen using from his condo balcony, watching the sky rather than other people's windows.

The odd thing was, Jason seemed to know that Phil knew all this about him, but he didn't question why. He just wanted to remove whatever bug it was that bugged Amy so he could go home and prove he was a stable genius. He rubbed his forehead. No, not that! Why did he think that? He just wanted to prove that Amy was wrong about him, that he was not an impotent whiner, that he was going to take positive action sometime very soon. Maybe next week. "So, how do you know you can debug me?" he repeated irritably.

"I've been at this a long time, Jason. I could determine from our phone calls that you don't have a serious psychiatric disorder; if I thought you did I would have referred you to someone else. I handle angst. Bugbears . . ."

"Muckraking. I haven't been mucked in a while. Is that included in the two-thousand-dollar fee?"

"Yes. You'll enjoy it. But let's take care of the money first, then we'll get started."

Jason counted out fifteen one-hundred-dollar bills, the amount still due after the five-hundred-dollar deposit check he mailed. The remainder had to be paid in cash. "It doesn't have to be rubles, does it?"

Phil grimaced. "No, no. Cold hard American cash works for me." Phil opened a desk drawer and slid the money into a manila envelope.

14

"Aren't you going to count it again?"

"I'm sure it's all there. I'll write you a receipt." Jason looked uncomfortable. "Do you want me to re-count it?" Phil asked.

"I'd feel better if you did." Jason watched him lay the money back out on the desk, bill by bill. "I thought of taking a picture of it," he said. "I'd have some proof in case you called me later and said I shorted you. But all you'd have to say is that I Photoshopped it."

"Well, now you'll have a receipt," Phil said, writing it. He tore it carefully along the perforated line and handed it over.

Jason read it twice. "Your name sounds familiar. I can't think where I heard it before."

Phil grinned. "My mother was a big fan of Magnum, P.I., you remember, that television series with Tom Selleck. That's my middle name. My last name is Willichuck."

"Really? I went to school with a guy named Willichuck. Duane Willichuck. He ate with his teeth."

"What do you mean?"

"You know, he didn't put the fork in his mouth and pull the food off with his lips. He put his teeth on the fork and it made this clicking scraping sound every time he took a bite. Even with soup on a spoon. Dribbled all over his chin, down his shirt. My God, I haven't thought of Dribble Duane in fifteen years."

15

"He's my father," Phil said.

"Are you shitting me?"

"Yes." Phil laughed. "Anyway, Phil Willichuck wasn't the badass shrink detective image I was going for in this neighborhood. Used to be called the Crosshairs District. It's the Inferno now." He sat forward. "Do you have a cell phone? Give it to me." He placed it inside the drawer with the money. "No phone calls, no texts, no outside communication for the next twenty-four hours."

"What if I have an emergency?"

"Reschedule it."

Jason glanced at the phone on the desk.

"Ringer's off," Phil said. "All my calls are going direct to voice mail."

Jason shifted nervously. This was already getting intense.

"All right, then," Phil began. "As I said, I don't believe you have a serious psychiatric disorder, so try to relax. It's all downhill from here. Bathroom's behind you, by the way. Door on your right."

"Figures."

"Let me ask you this first. Why do you think you're here?"

"Because Amy said she would dump me if I didn't show up."

"Who's Amy?"

"My girlfriend. Up until yesterday. She threw herself out."

16

"So, you don't want to be here. You're only doing this for her."

Jason shifted position. "No. Partly. I'm . . . I'm confused, I guess. Flustered. I don't understand why my opinions get on her nerves. I'm just pointing out all the crap going on now. Trump's election was like a drive-by shooting. I was hit but hanging on, praying for the exit wound. When he crowned himself emperor I lost it. I knew it was coming, I was worried about it, and then it happened—just like that it was a done deal. The Complicits just stood there clapping, grinning. They control everything now. I would have thrown up but I hadn't eaten yet. If I don't vent I'm going to explode."

"Amy disagrees with your views?"

"No, she agrees. She just thinks I talk about it too much if I'm not going to do anything. She acts like she's disappointed in me because I'm not down on the street being patriotic. That's pretty damn funny since she's the one who . . . well, never mind. She's got this view, this image in her head from Casablanca or Sound of Music, you know, where the patriots sing the national anthem right in the face of the enemy. All it would do is get my ass arrested. She knows the only patriotic music allowed now is Trump's new anthem—something about dawn's early tweets and broad hands and bright brains, some shit like that. She just wants to block all the bad stuff out and talk about *us*."

He covered his face. "Oh *gawd*, I *hate* that. What a fucking boring conversation. We get along great, she agrees we get along great, so why do we have to analyze it? I don't understand her. How can she not want to talk about all the dangerous shit going on? Jesus! We're officially a banana republic now. The whole world's on the brink of nuclear disaster. We've got Tweedle-Dee over there with a hydrogen bomb boner and Tweetie-Dumb lying in bed with his fries and cheeseburgers, jerking around with thermonuclear war. Call me neurotic but I think annihilation is kind of important.

"But she doesn't want to talk about any of that. That's "*depressing*." Let's just float around on some rosy sea of love and pretend the boat isn't sinking and a hundred sharks aren't waiting to roll our asses into sushi. I'm just trying to protect her. Us! I told her that, but she thinks I'm paranoid. Because I listen, because I pay attention, she thinks I need Viagra."

"Do you?"

"Need Viagra? No. I'm an animal. Sometimes I get distracted, that's all. It's a common problem with deep thinkers. My problem is I'm too alert."

"Who are the sharks?"

"The Complicits, hypocrites, bigots, the Bananas, the whole fucking regime. I just found out my downstairs neighbor is a Nazi nut. Skinny little Gordon Teasley! He knocked on my door and wanted to borrow a cup of tiki fuel. I can't trust anyone in my building, now. What I need is, I need to figure out how to rally followers and not get arrested for disturbing the Nazis. Be satirical, you know, like Saturday Night Live, but lead a double life like Bruce Wayne, except, you know, without the skills and money. It's hard being a charismatic leader when you have no recognizable qualities. Rebels need at least five followers to lead a revolt. It's taken me a year to get six on Twitter and three of those are bots. I can't be magnetic and funny with a two-hundred and eighty-character limit. That includes spaces. I get about halfway through a joke and there's no room left for the punchline. But that's not enough. I need to do more."

"You could join a march."

"Oh. You didn't get the tweet. Peaceful assembly is illegal now. Any reference to the Constitution is banned. The Complicits are working on Trump's new law of the land—Donald's Dictum. He's bragging already how really big it is. Did you hear him? *'Believe me,'* he says. *'It's the biggest Dictum ever in the history of Dictums.'*"

"So, what you're saying is, you want to be a rebel leader but don't know how."

Jason shifted uneasily. "No, that's not it. I want to be a . . . a debunker. I want to lampoon him. I want to deflate him. I want to mock and ridicule and expose him for the bloated lying selfish crook he is. Now he's changing our country name from America to Trumpssia—the National Loyalists of Trumpssia. You know what the irony is? During the Revolution the Loyalists were about one-third of the American population, about the same ratio of Trump supporters now. There's two-thirds more of us than them, so how did it even get this far, a crook like him? Donald Trump is pornography in a fat suit."

Jason sat forward, pointing his finger at Phil. "But here's our advantage. Trump's got an Achille's heel. He goes ballistic when people laugh at him. It eats him alive, but he can't leave it alone. He's addicted. He watches himself on three televisions at once, then replays the mockery over and over in his head. That's the beauty of it. He does it to himself. All we have to do is throw out the bait and watch him gorge on it until he's so unhinged the Complicits can't cover for him anymore. While they're killing each other to be the next emperor, we'll take our country back."

He leaned back and rubbed the back of his neck. "I know it would work. I know it! That's what I want to do, but I don't know how . . . where to start? It's unchartered territory. We've been sheep too long. There was a book out a long time ago, the sixties I think, A Nation of Sheep, the author was something Lederer. William. He warned we were letting other people think for us. We were being herded, even back them. Trump finally came along and divided us up like a stock yard, separate paddocks so we're easy to control."

"Jesus," Phil muttered.

"It's true. He's got the liberals in this pen and his base in that pen and the Wafflers in that pen and the wealthy but not filthy-wealthy in that pen and the don't-give-a-shits in that pen and they feed us what they need to control us, one fucking lie after another.   Divide and conquer. It's so basic it's embarrassing we let it happen. Now we've got those damn trucks on every corner." Jason got up and looked out the window. "There's one now, parking up the street. Have you seen what they hand out?"

"Not up close."

"Orange pods. The Bananas put them outside our bedroom windows. When we wake up we're one of them. Invasion of the pussy snatchers. Do you have a cigarette?"

"No. I thought you didn't smoke."

"I don't. Once in a while I just want to smell one. I chewed one once. It doesn't taste as good as it smells. It's like coffee beans. How can anything that smells so good in the bag be so nasty when you eat it?"

He peered up and down the street, checked the safety of his car, then sat back down. "Getting busy out there. When do the tanks start rolling in?"

"Later."

"I was kidding."

"Oh. Okay."

"You were serious? Tanks are actually going to drive up the street while I'm here?" Jason wrung his hands nervously. "Well yeah, that makes sense. It's called Donald's Inferno for a reason. Glad I didn't bother with the boat horn. I don't think I can honk my way out of here."

"Don't worry about it, Jason. It's just intimidation practice."

"Until the bombs hit. The CDC is having workshops now, how to survive a nuclear detonation. They've got radiation roadmaps, mushroom cloud pictures on their website, warnings not to lie outside in the afterglow. Everything you want to know about melting but were afraid to ask. My mother says she remembers when they had duck-and-cover practice in school back in the fifties. Trump takes over and we're diving under desks again. Tomorrow we might be circling Mars. They tell us to shelter in place but don't tell us where the place is."

Phil smirked. "Do you worry about it a lot, Jason?"

"About bombs? Not really. I'm pretty optimistic. I could die any one of a hundred horrible deaths. I don't want one of those out-of-body experiences, though; float close to the ceiling and watch doctors put those paddles on my chest and my body flops like a tuna. That would kill me. Seriously,

I'd have a heart attack watching that. But if I'm floating up there, then something's obviously wrong with me on the table, right? I was sucked out of my body for a reason. Am I shot? Stabbed? Was it voter cleansing? Will I make it into my forties? Am I old and bald or young and dead? Will I be an ethereal vapor or have a body I can actually feel with my own two hands? Does God allow feeling in the afterlife? If I'm dead, shouldn't I have something to look forward to? I don't know if I'll even make it to the gate. Trump's promising to build a huge wall between earth and heaven, two-thousand cubits long, keep all us undesirables out, everybody on their shithole country list. Evangelicals are going to pay for it"

Jason wrung his hands and sat back down. "If you could see my kidneys right now. My adrenal glands are in overdrive."

Phil sat in reflective silence several moments, then leaned forward and clasped his hands on the desk. "Jason," he said in a fatherly tone, "you have Weltschmerz."

Jason paled. "Shit! Incoming!" He ducked slightly. "Where did it come from? Is it a disease? How did I get it?"

"It's not a disease, Jason."

"Whew! Crap!" He clutched his left arm, looking faint. "Give me a minute."

"Weltschmerz is —"

"It doesn't have anything to do with this weird dent in my nose, does it? Because I can explain that."

"No, it's —"

"I was really self-conscious about my nose when I was a kid. I couldn't breathe without this embarrassing squeaking noise. It sounded like I was strangling a fairy. The doctor said I had a deviated septum. *Deviated*. That's so mean, sticking a moniker like that on a kid. My friends said they couldn't see it but I saw it every time I looked in the mirror. When I was ten I tried to straighten it with pliers."

Phil cringed. "Did it break?"

"No. I got this dent, though. My father made me sit on a sand pail for an hour, one of those kinds shaped like a castle. He said I was the King of Stupid. He could never understand the concept of self-experimentation and its role in medical research."

"Did you want to be a scientist, something in the medical field?"

"No. I wanted to find out if a septum could be un-deviated with pliers." He paused a second. "My father was a doctor."

"What kind?"

"Witch. Ha-ha. No. It's even better. He was a proctologist. A Rear Admiral. Have you heard the joke about the psychiatrist and the proctologist? A psychiatrist and a proctologist open an office in a small town and put up a sign that says, '*Dr. Smith* and Dr. Jones: Hysterias and Posteriors.' The town council doesn't like it and tells them they have to take it down. So, the doctors put up, 'Schizoids and Hemorrhoids.'

"The council has a fit so they change it to, 'Catatonics and High Colonics.' No way.

"How about, 'Manic Depressives and Anal Retentives.' Take it down!

"'Minds and Behinds?' No!

"'Lost Souls and Butt Holes.' Forget it!

"'Analysis and Anal Cysts.' Never!

"'Nuts and Butts?' Not a chance!

"'Freaks and Cheeks.' No way!

"'Loons and Moons?' Not happening.

"'Heads or Tails?' Better.

"Finally, the two doctors put up a sign that the town council finally accepts: 'Dr. Smith and Dr. Jones, Odds and Ends.'"

Phil chuckled. "Pretty good."

"Yeah. So what's Weltschmerz?"

"It's weariness of the world, Jason. World pain. It's the sadness and depression we feel when we think about all the evil in the world, all the social injustice and religious hypocrisy and phoniness. It can make us pessimistic about our future and we just want to fly out of here."

"Yeah, fight or flight, if we don't take any baggage. Airline fees are ridiculous. Trump's going to let them start charging for cabin pressure." He stared tiredly at the pigeon. "Did you see his tweet this morning? Sometimes I just want to stick an air-hose up my ass and get it over with."

Phil watched him closely. "You told me over the phone that your life is out of control."

"That's not what I meant. I think my life is in control. Everything else is screwed up. I don't have Weltschmerz. If I look depressed and weary it's because I couldn't eat anything this morning. I haven't slept in days except for a few long naps. Who can sleep when you don't know where to hide your money? My boss has a fucking picture of Trump's coronation next to my locker. I can't afford to quit. If the United States goes bankrupt, it'll lower my FICO score so my monthly peasant tithe will go up. If I don't pay it, I'll be evicted to one of Kushner's slumlord tenements.

"So yeah, I guess I'm pessimistic about my future. I started stockpiling cans of soup under the bed so I won't have to worry about starving for a while if I lose my job. Now I'm having nightmares that I can't find a can opener and I have to open a can with a hammer and a big nail. I get most of the way around and the lid collapses into the soup and when I stick in my finger to pull the lid back up, it gets cut on the jagged edge and I start bleeding and falling from a cliff to my death. Luckily I wake up before I hit bottom, but I'm always on the floor. The crazy thing is, I don't even like soup. I should be buying ravioli."

"When you —"

"What happens after Trump privatizes Fort Knox? *'Instead of the gold just lying there, it should be invested wisely, make more money for us, right?'* I hope it's true he can shit gold bricks. I heard he likes to roll around naked in his money. He throws it in the air and laughs and giggles and then his minions toss in a few cheeseburgers because it makes him happy when they squish. Then the laundered money is laundered again so Mueller can't trace it."

"Mueller was exiled."

"Yeah, that's right. One more thing I can't get my head around. You know what the national debt is now? Ninety-seven trillion. Why don't they just chop it up into little pieces and load it into Trump's golf carts? Or his shirt. His stomach already looks like a Clydesdale's ass. When he waddles around the golf course some of it could dribble out of his pants. Rush Limbaugh would eat it if we wrapped it in pie dough."

"When did —"

"Goodbye, America. It used to be great. Last one leaving, turn off the lights. Do you know where people are moving? Panama. I got *'The Gringo Guide for Dummy Expatriates.'* Panama's safer than Costa Rica and Guatemala. They have armed guards in the grocery stores and securing the beaches. Killing is bad for business down there. They don't want

America's reputation so the chances of being murdered are lower. If you're attacked you can call 1-0-4, but none of the operators speak English so you need somebody who can translate gunshots and screams for help."

"Do you—"

"I read that ISIS has no interest anymore sneaking into the United States. They're sitting outside the border taking notes on how Trump did it. Russia's still in charge of the hackings. I've got half a dozen security programs on my computer for all the different shit out there—spyware, adware, malware, hijacking, worms looking for weak places to penetrate my system, viruses hiding in my memory, reproducing, excreting code in my files, Trojans. Remember when they used to be fun? That reminds me, did you know men should sleep naked to protect their testicles? From infection. Briefs hold in the heat and moisture and bacteria. The cooler temperature also nurtures the sperm."

"That's good to know. When you say . . ."

"Anyway, every time I turn on my computer I'm harassed about installing updates. It's worse now since Trump started tracking us. I ignore it and ignore it and finally I cave and upgrade and my computer's totally fucked. Nothing works. Reboots, can't open or close anything, flashing screen. I can't move my fingers fast enough to satisfy my hard drive.

"When I finally do get online there's all this paranoia and bigotry and judgement and gnashing of teeth, and that's just the Evangelicals. I can't afford to get real information, not since net neutrality was axed." Jason pulled a folded paper from his pocket and opened it. "I brought this in case you haven't seen the new rates yet. Fourteen cents a month for Fox News," he read, "and nine-hundred seventy-two dollars and sixty-three cents a month to access CNN. Seven dollars a month for Pious Patriot, with a mandatory ten-dollar tithe, and eight-hundred fourteen dollars a month for NBC. Trump hasn't banned the networks yet because they're forbidden to talk about him. And he gets a huge cut."

"Do you need a glass of water, Jason?"

"No. Did you see the stock market dropped almost four-hundred points yesterday? After everyone else made millions I finally took the chance and invested and the market tanks. I can't handle the stress, up ten dollars one day, lose seventeen the next, gain three, lose six. It's like having sex in slow motion, the excitement, the collapse, working to get it back up. By the time you score it's not worth it anymore, you just want it over so you can go to sleep. I should diversify, but where? Under my bed? That's where I keep the soup. I'm thirty-four years old and I don't have a dime saved for retirement. Social Security is gone with the windbag.

"Yes, I'm a Millennial, but I'm not lazy and narcissistic like they say my generation is. I'm the opposite of narcissistic. I'm a Sagittarian. I'm generous and optimistic, even if I think we're hurtling toward destruction and mob rule.

"I get over-excited, and yes, I'm too blunt and talk too much and frequently offend people, but in a completely open, honest way. I can't help it if people are too stupid to see it."

—2—

Phil opened a desk drawer and retrieved a bottle of Tums. "You want one?"

"No, thanks. I took too many one time. My muscles started to twitch."

"Really?"

"Calcium carbonate overdose. You can't just pop them into your mouth like candy."

"I'll try to remember that." Phil casually popped two into his mouth and settled back into his chair. "Tell me about Amy."

"We had a huge fight last night. She said she would leave me if I didn't keep my appointment with you today. Then she said she was leaving me anyway. I never heard her yell so loud. She stormed out and *WHAM!* really slammed the door. When she didn't come back and didn't come back, I started getting chest pains. It was a good thing I took paramedic EKG and CPR courses last year. After I passed out I had to pound my chest three times and give myself mouth-to-mouth. My vital signs were so weak I passed out again."

"Okay, now you're yanking my chain."

"Maybe a little."

"Let's try to keep this real."

"My real or your real?"

"*Real* real. What was she mad about?"

"Flannel pants. All I said was,

"If the country goes bankrupt and L.L. Bean goes out of business, where will I buy flannel-lined pants?"

"It's summer, Jason," she said. "Don't worry about it."

"I'm not worried," he said. "I'm just thinking ahead. You know how cold my legs get."

"You are such a pessimist."

"No, I'm not. I'm just paying attention to what's going on."

She was ignoring him. He went for some sympathy. "You'd be pessimistic, too," he said, "if you got the note I got today."

"From who? Where?"

"At work. Harry Gumm slipped it anonymously into my pocket."

"Your boss? Do you have it? Let me see it." He gave her the folded Post-it note. "It's just the letter O," she said. "It's nothing. Literally, Jason, it's nothing."

"Yeah, that's what I thought at first. Then I saw it's not just an O. It's a deceptively cryptic zero. You can take it a hundred different ways, all of them

bad. *Somebody thinks I'm a big nothing? He's going to make my life hell until I renounce Obama? That I have zero chance keeping my job? That I will get zero sleep worrying about it?"*

"That you are totally Out of your Oxpecker, Ozone head?"

"Maybe."

She laughed scornfully. "Not 'maybe,' Jason. Overwhelmingly! I can't deal with your gloom and doom attitude anymore. You're so negative about everything. I'm sick of your constant bitching about Trump's regime if you're not going to do anything about it. If you put your cold feet in your big mouth, maybe something would change. I'm telling you, Jason, this is it! If you don't keep your appointment with Phil Magnum tomorrow, it's OVER! That's with a big, capitol O!

"No, on second thought, it's over now. You make me sick, Jason. Literally. I hate the person you've turned me into. I hate the person you've turned yourself into. You're on your own, you opinionated, obsessive . . . oxymoron!"

"A person can't be an oxymoron. I think you're overwrought," he said, but she was already out the door.

"She hasn't come back? Phil asked.

"Not as of seven this morning."

"Why do you think your boss doesn't like you?"

"Brains intimidate him. I don't have a crop of hair in my ears." Jason reached for a doughnut and took a bite. "He's your basic Trump minion in a crew cut. He wears the same outfit every day—argyle vest, argyle socks, khaki pants, brown vinyl lace-ups."

"Where do you work?"

Jason grimaced. "It's humiliating." He let out a deep breath, then said it. "Peeper's Sleepers. It's a mattress outlet store, closeouts, discontinued stuff. I make good commissions, though. That's the only reason I stay. Harry, my boss, he's the owner's son-in-law. He takes online courses at Trump's resurrected university. He just completed Mein Con: The Art of Distracting, Deflecting and Demoralizing. He practices every chance he gets."

"Like how?"

"He asks me stupid questions that don't have answers.

"*'Hey Jason, help me out here. How fast is a ball?'*

"*'I don't know, Harry. Is it a basketball or a baseball?'*

"*'Uh, a tennis ball.'*

"*'Fourteen,'* I said.

"*'That doesn't sound right,'* he says.

"*'Look it up,'* I said.

"Another time he asks, *'To the nearest dollar, how much is fifteen percent?'*

"*'Of what,'* I said.

34

"He says, *'Of anything. It doesn't matter. Fifteen percent is fifteen percent.'*

"'What's the circumference?' I said.

"'I'll get back to you,' he says. So he comes back and says, *'How many hours are in a banana?'*

"I said, *'A Banana soldier or a regular banana?'*"

"'Regular,' he said.

"I was tired. I said, *'I don't know, Harry.'*

"He says, *'That's why your time sheet is off.'*

"I said, *'Why do you keep screwing with me, Harry?'*

"He says, *'That sounds a little paranoid, Jason. I thought we were just having a conversation here.'* He holds up his hands and backs away from me. *'Just calm down, fella, okay? I'm not persecuting you.'*

"'Do Trumpballs ever get hard, Harry?" I said. *"Are they always just warm and fluffy in your pants? I'm just wondering.'"*

"Wow," Phil said. "He didn't fire you for that?"

"No. I make too much money for him."

"Why did you have to take a job like that? You said on the phone you graduated from Colorado State."

"I lost my job, got behind on my payments. It went on my credit report; the first thing employers look at. Then somebody broke the windshield on my car. I called the insurance company, but I decided to

35

just pay it myself, but the agent I talked to reported to CLUE that I might file a claim and that went on *that* report, and the insurance company raised my rates because I live in a high-risk zone since my windshield was smashed."

"I never heard of CLUE. What is it?"

"Comprehensive Loss Underwriting Exchange. It's a claims history of everything reported on us by insurance companies. We all have one. Underwriters look at that and our credit report and decide how much to screw us. Of course, now with Trump Insurance the mandatory national plan, that's all changing. Baby Face Eric controls the west coast, Don the Jr. runs the east coast operation, Pretty Girl Ivanka oversees the laundry."

Jason pitched his half-eaten doughnut into the wastebasket. "Do you have something cold to drink?"

The fridge was well stocked with juices, diet sodas, water, iced coffees. Jason tossed Phil a bottled water and chose orange juice for himself. For several minutes, they drank and listened to the muffled sounds of Twine Street shifting into high gear—the thrumming boom of car stereos, street riots, hissing tear gas, sirens—the plaintive saxophone threading it together like a swelling migraine.

"What kind of work did you do before the outlet store?"

"I was a federal workplace safety inspector for ten years, investigated workplace health hazards—

36

radiation, gasbag exposure, recognized and deflected bullshit, hazardous waste, suspicious odors, your basic deathtraps."

"Where was that?"

"American Food Supply."

"So, you were one of those inspectors who check how many bug parts are allowed per bite?"

"No, that's the EPA, or was. Trump deregulated it like everything else. Civil servants are government waste because they only serve the commoners." He glanced at the shipyard painting and the floor and his fingernails. "Yeah . . . so, my job was outsourced before the ax came down."

Which Phil knew was a lie. According to the file, he was fired. "How could they outsource the job to another country? You were checking workers checking American food."

"They caught me handing out FactCheck flyers."

"At work?"

He shrugged. "Sure. If they could stream Fox News into the break room, I could at least try to resuscitate their brains. They transferred me to Arizona, Jumbotron monitor near the border, catch and release immigrants trying to escape into Mexico. The exodus was hurting Trump's resorts. I was ordered to set up a job fair booth and hand out maps to Mar-a-Lago."

"*Real* real, remember?"

37

"I do better mixing it up. You're the detective. You can spot it. Amy spots it."

"Is she a Seattleite?"

"Oh yeah. Native."

"How long have you known her?"

"Since last winter."

"Do you live together?"

"Until last night."

"How did you meet?"

"Her family owns a bakery in Pike Place. McFine's Bakery. I was going by one day and saw her putting out a tray of bagels. She was completely the type I've always wished I deserve. Beautiful, long dark hair, Mona Lisa smile. She didn't actually look at me, but I sensed a definite mutual attraction. I started to open the door to go in but then I had a wave of panic. What if she voted for Trump? I could forgive her if she did—a lot of people made that mistake and were in therapy, but what if she didn't regret it? What if she was one of the thirty-five percent? She didn't look brainwashed, but who can see the truth when you're falling in love? She went back into the kitchen, but I knew I had to find out. I swallowed my fear and went in.

"An old lady was working behind the counter. I browsed around casually, checked out a rack of pastry, tried not to look hungry and desperate and needy. After a couple minutes the girl came back out. The old lady whispered something to her, then she

38

left. I strolled around, scared shitless I'd say something stupid."

"Can I help you find something?" the girl said.

"Do you have chocolate éclairs?"

"I'm sorry, we sold them all this morning. If you want to place an order I can have them here for you tomorrow morning."

"Okay."

"How many?

"A dozen. Twelve."

"Custard cream with chocolate glaze?"

"Perfect."

She wrote quickly on a notepad. "Your name?"

"Uh . . ." He cleared his throat. "I'm sorry, what did you say?"

"What is your name? So nobody else will buy your order." She smiled up at him.

He could not remember his name. He couldn't even remember what letter it started with. It was worse than his worst, worst nightmare. Just turn around and run. Run, Jason! In a miraculous flash, there it was.

"Jason," he said. "Jason Nickle." He spelled it out, cringing from the waver in his voice. He couldn't hear the words but she was writing and not looking nervous, wary of him.

He was sweating, a muscle in his forehead jumping like an electrified snake. The old lady came out of the back room and pretended to dust the counter, glowering at him. She finally noticed she forgot the dust cloth. She curled her lip at him, gave him a 'watch it, buddy' head jerk and shuffled back behind the door.

"It's okay, Nana," the girl said. She glanced up at him and smiled, as if to say, 'I'm sorry, just ignore her.' Jason felt his heart melt into his chest cavity.

He cleared his throat. "Has this store been here long?" He knew it had been; he had just never been inspired to go in before.

"Thirty-nine years," she said, with pride.

"Are you a McFine?"

"I'm Amy. My parents started the store right after I was born."

He did some quick math. She couldn't be . . .

"Kidding!" she said, laughing.

A small group of teenage girls came in, all wearing Florida Gator jackets, carrying souvenir bags they'd lugged up from the waterfront. "Do you have pastelitos?" one of them asked. "They're Cuban pastries," she added, certain Amy wouldn't know what she was talking about. She cast a smug look back at her friends, who stifled smirks.

"Yes, I know," Amy said. "They're puffed up tarts."

"Well, kind of," the girl stammered.

"No, we don't have those. We have cappuccino mousse timbales. They're puffy."

The girl looked nervously at her friends. "We'll think about it, okay?" She flashed a huge fake smile. "Tha-a-a-nks!"

"You're wel-come," Amy sang back. "Thanks for stopping in."

Jason wanted to grab her and kiss her right then. Beauty. Spunk. Humor. The fates couldn't be so cruel as to make her a xenophobic Trumpet. She looked at him as if to ask, 'Did you want anything else?' He tried to read her body signals. Did wiping her hands on her apron mean she wanted him to stay and talk longer? Was her blank expression merely a mask to hide her own inner turmoil and, hopefully, fire? God, she was good at it. He couldn't read a damned thing.

"Okay then," he said, stepping backward. "I guess I'll see you tomorrow."

"Yes." She smiled. "I'll be here."

"If I think of anything else, I'll call."

"Okay."

"The timbales sound good."

"They are. Would you like one?"

"No thanks. I just had breakfast." He mentally kicked himself. Just had breakfast? It was two in the afternoon! For God's sake, Jason, think before you speak!

41

"Okay then, well, see you tomorrow." He backed out of the store and blended into the heavy stream of tourists flowing through the market corridor.

Even in winter Pike Place Market was always crowded but he loved the energy of the place, the insane variety of colors, the complex smells, the seaport air. Trump's deregulation of poisons and noxious toxins hadn't rolled in yet, so everyone was smiling and breathing without coughing and turning green.

Jason ambled through the crowd past stalls of dried flowers and stands of fresh produce, past quirky shops selling teas and herbal tranquilizers, bulk spices and essences and weed. He stopped as he always did at the fish mart and stared at the rows and piles and stacks of fish and seafood on sheets or buckets of crushed ice, the massive scallops, massive crab legs, massive prawns. He wandered on, preoccupied, maneuvering around baby carriages and couples in love, holding hands, stupidly happy. "Did you watch the news today?" he casually asked one couple. "Huh?" the guy replied.

"That's my problem," Jason thought as he strolled and stewed. "I need to be a tourist more often, take a vacation from being an informed voter. He should get a cup of coffee and sit on that bronze pig over there and just watch people going by, study the ones wearing red MAGA caps. Maybe

he could discern some physical clue he could compare to Amy, some vacuous look behind the eyes, some fish-puckering tendencies around the lips.

Oh, this is ridiculous! Just go back and find out! But be subtle about it, clever, so she won't suspect your true motives. Just buy a timbale and take your time.

"Hi!" he said, popping his head into the bakery. She looked startled to see him, then smiled the faint smile, the Mona Lisa smile.

"I was just wondering," he said, closing the door behind him, "who did you vote for?"

"I beg your pardon?"

"I was wondering who you voted for, in the last presidential election."

She stared at him. "That's none of your business. A person's vote is very personal and private."

"Oh yeah, I understand. I never tell strangers who I voted for. We have that in common. But I'm, uh, I'm taking a poll."

"For who?"

"Me."

She shook her head. "I don't understand. Why do you care who I voted for?"

"Because I want to ask you out to dinner and we couldn't enjoy ourselves if we didn't know if we were compatible, politically I mean. I don't want to

43

waste your time if there's a chance we could hate each other after we ordered. Like, I could mention I want to preserve the planet and you might say you want to sell it on Ebay. I could be a journalist, you would want to put me in prison. I think morals matter in a president . . ."

"Yes okay, I get your point." She thought a moment. "Well, actually, I didn't vote."

He stared a moment, then let out his breath. "Okay! Well . . . okay then. But if you had voted, who would you have been closest to voting for?"

"Probably Bernie Sanders. Who did you vote for?"

"I wrote in Biden. Yeah, I know, I blew my vote. Who knew a misogynist liar would be so popular? So . . . would you have dinner with me tonight? If you think you might be hungry. Or tomorrow night. I usually want to eat by then."

She tucked a lock of glossy hair behind her ear, thinking, staring intently at him. "Okay. Sure. I don't finish here till six."

"Meet you at Matt's?" It was just upstairs. Familiar. Close. Safe.

The wheels were turning. "Okay. It'll be a few minutes after."

The old lady stuck her head out the kitchen door, glaring at him. "Your éclairs aren't ready yet!" she barked at him.

"He knows, Nana. It's okay."

"And she showed up," Phil said.

"She showed up. It was perfect for a while, until it started heading south."

"Any particular reason?"

"Yeah. Me. In the beginning we talked about everything, the crap going on in the world, politics, games, movies. It was great. It was better than . . . no, not better than that, but close. There was no question in my mind, she was my soul mate. She understood everything I worried about, she was interested in everything I said, asked a million questions. It was such a high. I couldn't believe I was so lucky.

"Every Wednesday she has this routine, she's done it for years, she takes the Bainbridge ferry over and back before dark, no matter what the weather is, watches the sunset, or the greyset, then the city skyline coming back, the lights coming on. I'd never done that, just to do it. Have you?"

"I have, yes."

"We freeze our asses off sometimes; most of the time we hang out on the upper deck. In the beginning she thought I was the funniest guy on the planet."

"No seriously," he said. "When I die, who has dibs, God or Visa? If I owe money on my card, do they have a right to sell my body parts?"

"Oh Jason, that's so gruesome!" But she was laughing, hugging his arm. A cold drizzle began to fall. He reached over and pulled the hood of her rain jacket up over her hair. She laid her head against his shoulder. For several minutes they watched a pod of orcas playing in the wake of a speedboat.

"To answer your question," he said, "yes, I believe in God. The resurrection of the dead scares me, though. All the hypocrites will come back as Evangelicals."

"Were your parents religious?"

"Oh yeah, very religious. It was a religion. I'm not sure what it was—one of the egomaniacal dogmas. They knew Satan's last name. I was sprinkled eight or nine times, but it rolled off. My Aunt Brisky came over to the house and said that sprinkling didn't count. I was about eight then, old enough to be accountable for my sins. I assumed that meant things like playing with my wiener."

When Amy stopped giggling, he went on. "She raised hell—I mean literally, I was going to hell—unless I was fully dipped. She set it up with her pastor to dunk me the next Sunday, but it had to be at high tide. She said when she walked in mud, her shoes made a dirty sucking sound that made her vagina twitch.

"When I went to bed that night, I had a terrible nightmare. I was standing somewhere on the edge of Puget Sound, cold water up to my waist, wearing

46

a white hospital gown. There was a crowd of people standing on the bank watching me. There was a man next to me wearing a purple robe with an orange sash and red earmuffs. He put his arm around me and told me to hold my breath. I plugged my nose and as I was being lowered my heart started to pound violently because I was afraid the gown would float open in back and I was naked underneath. But then somebody standing on the shore yelled, 'He's a democrat!' and everything changed.

"The man in the red earmuffs raised me back up and said, 'Is that true?' and I said, 'I don't understand. You accept Trump and he's a pussy grabber.' And he said, 'Yes, he's rated PG. You're an FD, my son.' I said, 'What's that?' and he said, 'A fucking democrat.' I yelled, 'Vive la Gore!' and ran out of the water and up a hill while the whole village chased me with pitchforks and torches. All I kept thinking was, 'What would Jesus do?'"

"Trump and Gore weren't in the picture when you were eight."

"It was a prophetic dream. It all came true, except for the dunking part."

The ferry was making the return run from Bainbridge Island. The passengers who worked in Seattle had disembarked; the deck was beginning to fill with tourists.

"Do you want coffee?" he asked.

47

"No. You can't bring it out here." She stared at the approaching skyline. "I can't believe you've never been married. The saying is so true, you know, at my age all the good guys are married or gay."

"I'm definitely bilateral. Both sides of me want to grab your ass."

"You do it so well."

"I can't take any credit. It's involuntary. You don't know the hell I went through holding off till our second date."

"Third date. You grabbed my ass on our third date."

"I grabbed your ass on our second date, in the park. Our first date was dinner at Spinasse."

"Our first date was at Matt's."

"That wasn't really a date."

"Of course it was. What else was it?"

"The pre-date interview. You had to prove to your Nana I wasn't a pervert. She warned you, right? What noun did she use?"

"I don't remember."

"Oh, come on. Yes, you do. What did she call me?"

"A degenerate asshole."

Jason laughed loudly.

"It wasn't personal, Jason. She calls every man I meet the same thing. She had a very unhappy marriage. What do you mean, pre-date interview?"

"Screening, see if I qualified for a date. We weren't texting so you had to find out. Matt's was it. I was sweating the questions—Could I provide you with a demonstration of my best work in a discreet yet mind-blowing way. How was I different from the competition. Would I be willing to participate in text sex . . ."

"I didn't suggest anything close to that!"

"Yeah, well, there were signals; the way you brushed your finger over an app, your interaction without actually unlocking, the residue of oil on the screen as you repeatedly stroked your finger. I couldn't walk for a week."

They watched the lights of the city grow richer and brighter, a brilliant expanding postcard with clear views of the Space Needle and Great Wheel. The air was windless, cool and salty.

"Great Christmas for Putin this year," Jason said. "He got his very own Santa Claus into the White House. Sabo Tage and his faithful reign-deer, Scammer and Grifter and Bully and Bigot. To the top of the torch! to the top of the wall! Now slash away! Slash away! Slash away all!"

She looked concerned. "This really bothers you, doesn't it."

He shrugged. "I keep it in perspective. That's north of here, near Bellingham. Don't worry. It won't be a problem."

49

—3—

"Every time I watch those old movies with Arnold Schwarzenegger, 'True Lies' and like that, I really connect with his character, psychologically. He can crush anybody with two words. Did you see Terminator 2? He stands up naked and scares the shit out of every rat in L. A. I should look up who the scriptwriters were, have them write me some one-liners. I'd love to look a Banana in the face and say something like, *'You're peeled, banana boy.'* Except I'd get a fist in my face. I'd be dead before I hit the floor. I'm a bleeder. I have to take a lot of aspirin."

"Why?"

"To stop heart attacks."

"How many have you had?"

"None so far. That's why I take aspirin."

"Do heart attacks run in your family?"

"Not for long. They drop dead."

"Who in your family?"

"My father, for one."

"I'm sorry. How old was he?"

"Sixty-two."

"A lot older than you."

"He didn't have him for a father."

"When did he die?"

"Two years ago. It was very . . . quick."

"What was he doing?"

"Watching TV. Fox News forgot to warn that some footage would be too graphic for some viewers. It was a clip of Obama's speech on human rights. His last words were, *'Card carrying commie!'* and he dropped dead. He would have worshipped Trump."

"What kind of childhood did you have?"

"It was average, I guess. I've blocked out most of it. My parents were wealthy, *extreme* right wing. Before my father died, maybe even after, he was fighting to *'Impeach the antichrist!'* When I was sixteen he caught me in my bedroom closet watching a show about Greenpeace, out there on the ocean in these rubber rafts, between the whales and the harpoon ships. He grabbed my ear and dragged me out of the closet and yelled, *'Tell the truth! Are you a tree hugger?'* I said, *'Yes! I am! I'm tired of hiding who I am. I care about the environment, okay? I'm bipartisan!'* He never looked at me again. Whenever I went into the same room he was, his mustache started to twitch. It looked like a mouse humping his upper lip. I wanted to whack it with a flyswatter."

Phil smirked. "It scared the shit out of you, didn't it."

"What do you mean?"

"When he dropped dead. No warning."

"I don't know. Maybe. I don't remember."

"Did you go to the funeral?"

"Oh yeah. I was there for my mother. She wanted the best; bronze deluxe casket, pillow-top mattress, adjustable headrest, memory tube."

"Memory tube. What's that."

"It's a glass tube about three inches long, half inch in diameter. It screws into the end of the casket. The funeral home puts the person's identity in it in case there's a flood and the casket pops out of the ground. You can also put in a personal note to your deceased loved one, some reading entertainment while they're floating down the river."

"Did you?"

"What?"

"Put in a note?"

"No." He smirked and looked toward the window. The pigeon was gone. "Do you hear that rumbling noise?"

"Yeah. Just tune it out."

"What is it? Aren't you curious?" He got up to look out the window.

"I wouldn't," Phil said.

"Why not?" Jason paled and dropped back into his chair.

"The Bananas are out patrolling now. "It's just a good idea not to expose yourself."

52

"I thought you said they're too yellow to come up here."

"They are. But if they're bored they'll wait downstairs for you to come out."

The rumbling grew louder. "What is that?" Jason asked. "Is it the tanks?"

"Probably."

"I heard they have big guns on them. That's what Trump said. *'The biggest guns you ever saw. Believe me.'*"

"I don't know about that. They're large caliber cannons."

"But why? What for? We're just sitting here eating donuts. We're not doing anything."

"It's a show of force, Jason. That's all. Trump does it to keep us scared and in line. Discourage dissenters."

"Who drives them? Our military?"

"No-no. No. They refuse. That's the only funny part of all this. Trump hasn't found a way to make them obey yet. The Bananas are building their own Army. And they're recruiting."

Jason glared at the painting. "Yeah. Amy and I had our first fight about this. We were at Henry's, after a Seahawks game. The server just brought some Gorgonzola fries."

She punched his arm. "Stop feeling up my thigh, Jason." But she didn't move away.

53

She bit into a waffle fry drizzled in creamy gorgonzola cheese sauce, closed her eyes and groaned. "Oh my god, these are so good. Oh. Um-m-m. Wait till you taste these, Jason. This is the best batch ever." She took another bite, savoring every morsel.

Jason sat watching her. "Do you know that every time you eat something you love, you groan like you're having sex?"

"I thought we were done talking about sex."

"We are. This is just an observation."

"I can't help it. This is . . .oh . . . this is so-o good I can hardly stand it." She moaned softly, smacking her lips.

He glanced around uneasily. No one was paying attention to them. "It's kind of embarrassing," he said anyway.

"I don't care. I enjoy food. I enjoy life. When something goes into my body that's this good, I groan, Jason."

Which was true. He felt very manly in bed.

"Here," she said. "Take a bite."

"M-m-m-m." he said, chewing. "Yeah. It's tasty."

"You are such a fake," she scowled. "That's okay. Never mind. I'll enjoy it enough for both of us." She took another crunchy bite and rolled it over her tongue, exposing the flavors to all her taste buds like a wine connoisseur. "Not too starchy, light

weight, crisp texture with a hint of russet and . . . canola."

She pursed her lips as though to whistle, breathed through her mouth and exhaled through her nose.

"What are you doing?"

"Liberating the aromas. Oh. There's a wave of sea salt, Mediterranean . . . from the Guérande region of France . . . "

"Okay. I get it." He smirked and sipped his beer. "I'm just saying, I can enjoy food as much as the next person without sounding like I'm close to an orgasm."

"Really, Jason?" She stopped eating and dabbed her mouth with a napkin. "Really?" Her left eyebrow arched. "Actually, Jason, sometimes I don't think you enjoy an orgasm when you're having one. I think you're thinking about something else. I think you're always thinking about something else."

"What do you mean? That's . . . it's not humanly possible to think about something else when your brain is exploding. It takes me five minutes to peel it off the ceiling. Trust me, Amy, there's no way I'm going anywhere else when I'm coming. Why would you even say something like that?"

She shrugged. "You just always seem preoccupied."

"With what?"

"How should I know? Your health. Politics. Trump. Armageddon. You worry a lot. You're a worry wart, Jason."

He didn't feel like arguing. "I get nervous when I can't find my glasses."

"You don't wear glasses."

"I would if I could find them. What is astigmatism anyway? Does it mean I have a stigma?"

"It means your eye is shaped like a football instead of a basketball. Don't worry about it. Yours are shaped like aspirin."

"Really? This morning I thought they looked like acetaminophen caplets. I'm allergic. I get blisters and the skin loosens inside my mouth."

"Dodging-dodging-dodging-dodging-dodging."

"I'm not dodging. I don't even remember what we were talking about."

"We were talking about your preoccupation with everything else except us."

"We were? Was I here?"

"Probably not."

He picked up a waffle fry and popped it into his mouth. "Ohmygod, you're right. This is amazing. Oh yeah, baby. I gotta have more like this. That one right there. Yeah. That's it. Oh man. I love you, Amy. I love you."

56

"Not funny. You're just doing it again. Every time I ask you something you don't want to answer, you dodge. You joke. You change the subject. Why don't we just talk about this, Jason? You. Are. A. Worry. Wart."

He frowned and stared out the window. "I wouldn't call it worry.Disturbed, maybe. Alarmed's a little closer. Panicky probably nails it." He pulled out his cell phone. "I need to check something."

"You just checked fifteen minutes ago."

"I know, but something might have happened since then. My veins start to ache if I don't get a news fix." He scanned several recent posts. "Maybe Trump tweeted something impeachable this time. I don't understand what's taking Mueller so long. People die a slow death faster than this investigation. How many corruptions does he need? Maybe that's been Trump's modus operandi all along, you know, be so massively corrupt the investigators are buried in it. Mueller has to hurry. It's getting more dangerous every day."

"What do you mean?"

"Trump is turning the United States into bananaland, a banana republic. The frog thing is happening right now."

"What frog?"

"Us. We're the frog. We're in a slow boil, Amy. Our goose is cooked."

"I thought the metaphor was a frog?"

57

"He croaked. That's how fast this is happening. Trump wants to be a dictator. His holes pucker every time he gets around a fascist. That squirrely, dreamy face he gets with Putin? That's not a grin. He's having an orgasm. Putin's got a pimp and we've got a puppet clown working the stage. Make 'em laugh. Make 'em clap for more, orf-orf-orf!

"'I am the greatest president since . . . ever! . . . since Columbus crossed the Delaware in that little boat. If it had been my boat it would have been a much bigger boat, believe me. When it landed on Plymouth Rock I would have made a deal with the Indians and there would have been no Indian wars taming the west because we would have owned the west already. I would have made the deal. Crooked Hillary couldn't have done that. We wouldn't be a continent now if I hadn't won massively. Now I have to clean the swamp. The courts, the judges, they're all rigged, a bunch of Barack Hussein lovers and illegals raping and murdering my rule of law I just passed. I will clean the swamp of Deep State institutions. I have absolute authority to do that. The courts, the FBI, the other intel—and let me tell you, folks, they're too inintelligent to be intelligent. We need to purge the FBI!_Eject them all! Like it says in the Bible—purge is actually in the Bible, did you know that? I bet you didn't know that. In the King James chapter it says, purge every branch!

We're going to Make America Great Again and throw out the enemy of people, FAKE NEWS! Smack 'em-down! Lock 'em up! Beat the shit out of 'em! I'll pay your legal bills. Yey! YEYYYYY!'"

The restaurant had grown silent; everyone was staring at him. Jason dropped his arms and waited until normal murmuring resumed.

"Well that wasn't embarrassing," Amy said.

"That's how it happens, Amy," he said a few decibels lower. 'Don't pay any attention to those oligarchs behind the curtain.' They're pulling the strings and working the money machines, ka-ching ka-ching. We're the chings. They're the one-armed bandits and we're the little old ladies in Vegas hooked up to glucose monitors pumping and sweating for a win, ten bucks a pull. We pump in five thousand bucks and every two weeks the machines kick out tokens. The Complicits and Vipers are praying the sleeping giant never wakes up."

"Oh, I don't know, Jason," she said tiredly. "That's sounds so negative. So defeatist. Who are the Vipers?"

"Evangelicals. White-washed Vipers."

"I think it was 'white-washed tombs' and 'brood of vipers.'"

"Exactly. Tombs and Vipers. They're right in there with Trump's machine, raking it in. This is how banana republics work. Everything is *operated like a private business. All the profits go to the ruling class. That's why Trump and his cronies want to privatize prisons and armies and Social Security.*

"This isn't a movie, Amy. This shit is happening! Trump wants to sell our national assets to pay for his infrastructure plan—airports, power assets like TVA and Bonneville, highways, parkways, water aqueducts. He's already chopping environment protections to make it easier. Regulations aren't profitable. He wants private companies to operate them, his corporate buddies, charge God knows what to use them. Maybe France will buy back the Statue of Liberty.

"The Complicits will blow through whatever purchase money they get. If you sell off your assets you end up going broke because the money's not coming in anymore, so what happens then? You file for bankruptcy—Trump's specialty!

"They're doing that with public lands right now, making them private. Look what Trump's already doing to national monuments, cutting off millions of acres of land for commercial development. You know what he said? 'We will usher in a bright new future of wonder and wealth.' Wealth, Amy. For them, after Trump skims his off the top. They get the money and we get the bill. We the People have to pay it, not them. Banks and corporations are above the law now. Just like a banana republic ruled by a

family. You want to know why the Complicits are blind and deaf and lie and cover for him? Because anything goes if it makes them money. Trump will sign anything they put in front of him. He just wants to grin and show off his signature and get richer. They're working together now but pretty soon it's going to be every Complicit for himself."

"Who are the Complicits?"

"Politicians, oligarchs he launders money for, corporate backers, lobbyists. Don't ever look in their eyes, Amy. They're lifeless, you know, like a shark, black eyes, doll's eyes. When they bite you, the eyes roll over white and all you hear is that terrible high pitched screamin' . . ."

"Oh for god's sake, shut up, Jason. I don't know why you love that Jaws part so much."

"It's funny. That's what comedy is, tragedy plus time. When Trump does time, we'll all laugh. Did you ever notice he never laughs? There's a Greek word for it—agelastas. It means un-laugher. Even chimpanzees laugh. On the tree of life diagram in The Evolution of Man, man is at the top of the tree with chimpanzees a little way under that. Further down are the semi-apes and pouched animals. Somewhere in that area Trump fell out of the tree and hit his head and got a deferment from serving in the human race. Did you know he thinks pets are low class?"

"Are the people who voted for him the Complicits?"

"No. They're either Basers or Wafflers, the ones who switch back and forth. Novos didn't vote at all."

"So, the KKK and the neo-Nazis and the supremacists, they're Basers?"

"No. They're Scums. They'll be Trump's army when the banana republic takes over. Our military won't do it. Navy Seals will put a shark in his bathtub. Trump's terrified of them. He'll jump out and run naked down the street and a homeless dog will bite him in the ass."

"What are the resisters, the opposition called?"

"I don't know yet. I thought of Trueps, like for true patriots. Maybe the Ones. Like what Obama said in his speech, 'We are the Ones we've been waiting for.' Alice Walker wrote a book with that title, too. I think it goes back to a Hopi prophesy. Anyway, it says it." He ate a fry. He felt tired. "Do you want to go home and fool around?"

"I don't think so, Jason. I'm not in the mood. All this talk about banana republics is kind of depressing. Maybe we should take a walk."

"And so it begins," he muttered."

"What do you mean?"

"Nothing," Jason replied.

"What did you mean?" Phil asked. "And so *what* begins?"

"The cool-down. She was starting to lose interest. They all do. Something about me eventually turns women off. I know I'm not a babe-magnet, but I don't think I'm bad looking. Do you?"

"No. Not at all. If I was a woman I think I'd be attracted."

"Really? That kind of surprises me. I think of myself as pretty generic looking. Generic Jason. The only thing that gets me anywhere is my sense of humor. If I can make them laugh in the first couple minutes, I have a chance.

"There was this one girl I met in a singles bar. She was hot but man, what a deadpan. I got a few smirks out of her but no laughs. I'd bought her three drinks and asked if she wanted to go to her place, or my place, or someplace. She looks me up and down and says, *'I only have organic sex. I don't put anything into my body that isn't organic.'* I said, *'It's gluten-free.'* She says, *'Is it a GMO?'*"

"What's that?" Phil asked.

"It means, genetically modified organism. It's a big issue now. I said to her, *"Will you care, afterward?"*"

"What happened?"

"We went to her place. I never saw her after that. I don't know who dumped who. I'm usually the dumpee"

"Amy's lasted quite a while."

"Yeah."

"Is she your longest relationship?"

"Yeah. The second longest lasted about three months. Trisha. She had a dog, Dozer. I think it was a dog. It was the size of a refrigerator. He didn't like me. Every time he saw me his tail shot up in the air and switched back and forth, like a metronome, ticking off the time till he could rip out my throat. We didn't move in together, but I practically lived at her place. What was that line from Moonstruck, Cher and Nicholas Cage getting it on the first time, she says something about just leaving the skin on her bones. That's how it was with us. Just raw animal passion at first."

"The best kind."

"Tell me. We were ripping clothes off with our teeth. That lasted about a month, then it was normal passionate sex every day, then passionate sex every other day, then sex a couple times a week, then . . . zip. Zilch. I asked her about it and she mishy-mouthed about it at first."

"I'm just tired lately."

"Yeah, I know. You're getting too much sleep."

"We have different needs," she said. "I don't want sex every day."

"Is this a Biblical day, as in, one day is as a thousand years? Because that's what it feels like."

"I don't like this pressure, Jason. I don't appreciate it and I don't deserve it."

"What pressure? I'm just asking you about it, that's all. You have a king-size bed with a two-hundred-pound dog that sleeps between us now like a sack of concrete. I couldn't move that dog with a forklift. How do I know? Because I've tried. Dozer bit my hand last night. Do you know that? Look at these bruises! He almost drew blood."

"Well of course he bit you. Everybody knows you're not supposed to shove a dog off the bed when they're sleeping."

"He tries to shove me off first! For the last week I've woke up with his claws in my back and he's pushing me over the edge. Can you seriously tell me you haven't heard the kicking and screaming before I hit the floor?"

"I heard. I was hoping you'd take the hint and hit the road." And then the mortal wound: "You're not as great in bed as you think you are, Jason."

He didn't flinch. "I'm sorry you feel that way," he replied. "Too bad about the RAV4."

"What RAV4?"

"It's your birthday tomorrow. You figure it out."

"You bought her a car?" Phil asked.

"No. She's always wanted a RAV4. I just said it to drive her crazy. I couldn't think of a comeback for the bed slam. My ego was pretty shot." He stared out the window and smirked.

"She called me the next day asking about it. "It's beside the point now," I told her. "I sold it."

—4—

Phil opened a bottom desk drawer and removed a plastic bottle of rubbing alcohol, a cotton ball and a couple small envelopes. "Are you sweaty?" he asked.

"A little."

Phil dampened the cotton ball with alcohol and walked around the desk. "Hold out your wrist. Turn it over."

"What are you doing?"

"I'm going to put on a temporary tattoo. Don't worry, it's water-based ink." He rubbed a patch the size of a half-dollar on the inside of Jason's wrist with the damp cotton ball. "Blow on it." He tore open one of the small envelopes.

"What's this for?"

"It's a replica of Trump's insignia. Can't buy and sell without it. Sometimes a Banana's outside the restaurant. They don't half look so don't worry about it. Just flash it casually like you've done it a hundred times and go on into the restaurant."

"My god," Jason uttered.

Phil carefully peeled the clear backing off the transfer, an orange grinning head wearing an olive leaf wreath, and pressed the image face down on the cleaned skin. "Don't move." He quickly ripped open a wet-wipe and pressed it over the tattoo. "This just takes a minute. You can wash it off tomorrow when you get home."

"I heard this was happening," Jason said. "It hasn't hit my neighborhood yet." The seconds ticked by. "What does it say? 'In Trump We Trust?' 'One Nation Under Putin?' 'E Pluribus Asshole?'"

"I don't know, I never read it." Phil carefully peeled back a corner of the paper. "Good. It took. Don't touch it, I forgot something." He dropped the wet paper into the wastebasket, removed a dry-powder spray bottle from the desk and spritzed a light fog of talcum powder over the fresh tattoo. "This gives it a more natural look, dulls it down." He smiled at his creation. "Just one more thing and we can go." He removed two gas masks from the bottom drawer and handed one to Jason. "You don't need to put it on. Just hold it, in case."

"In case of what?" Jason followed him out the door. "In case of *what*?" he repeated. "Where's lunch, Afghanistan?" Partway down the stairwell, Jason remembered the spider.

"There's a black widow spider on that step," he said, looking two steps further down.

"Oh yeah?" Phil was below it. "Yes, I see it there. Thanks." He turned and continued down the stairs. Jason hugged the opposite wall and was quickly behind him. When Phil opened the door, the pigeon ambled in from the sidewalk.

"This is Drake, my assistant," Phil said. "He watches the place for me. If something's going on he thinks is a threat to me, he taps on the window. Drake," he said to the bird, "eat the spider." He closed the door, leaving the bird inside.

The transformation of Twine Street in four hours was shocking; blaring horns and emergency sirens, acrid smoke drifting from unseen fires, homeless milling about aimlessly or curled up on the sidewalks, the hard stares from hardened men standing in small groups on every corner. Jason was relieved to find his pet Prius still intact, not the picked clean carcass he fully expected.

As though reading his mind, Phil said, "Nobody will bother it as long as it's inside the yellow markers. They know you're my client."

An Asian teenager yelled from across the street, "Who's the fool, brain man?" His fellow gang-members laughed loudly.

"Standard greeting," Phil muttered to Jason. "Hey, Deshi!" he yelled back. "Where's your hooptie?"

"Gettin' a spray job."

"What color?"

"Lime green. Match my duck tape!"

"I thought your duck tape was red."

"That's the bumper, Sherlock. This is the driver door."

When they were well past, Jason asked, "What's a hooptie?"

"It's a piece of shit car, clothes hanger holding up the tail-pipe, backfires when it's turned off, mismatched tires, spinning plastic hubcaps, hot-glued mirrors, the gaudier and more embarrassing to drive, the better."

"Psst!' someone hissed loudly. "Psst! Hey! Over here."

Jason stopped and looked around. A grizzled old man shuffled toward him. "Yeah *you,* dumb shit. Who else would I be pssting at?" He looked both ways then slyly opened his coat. "I got some fresh." He withdrew an orange tablet from an inside pocket.

Jason stared at it. "I'm not into drugs."

"This ain't drugs, you stupid bastard. This is Spraytan Orange. It ain't just a spray anymore. This is pure delusion, straight from Kushner's 666 tower. Finally made that place profitable," he cackled. "Come on. Try it. Gimme a buck and the first one's free. Believe me, you won't give a shit about nothin' or nobody. It's all going to be just about you."

"Let's go," Phil said.

Jason ignored him. "Why would you give it to me free, not counting the buck?"

"I'm on commission, see? I get a meal for every new convert." He glanced quickly toward an upper window across the street. "They're watchin' me right now, make sure I don't eat it myself. Here. Take it." It was the size of a half-dollar, embossed with the same grinning image as the tattoo.

Jason backed off. "No thanks."

"Don't be an asshole," the man said. "They're gonna get you sooner or later. When you gonna wise up? This is the zone now. That other world's long gone. Dearly departed U. S. of A." He cackled again, then looked around nervously.

"Come on," Phil said.

"Can't keep him moral forever, dickhead," the old man shouted after them.

"That kill your appetite?" Phil asked.

"No. All I've had today was that half donut. Did you ever taste a Spraytan?"

"I broke off a piece once and put the tip of my tongue on it. It's potent. For a minute I felt what a narcissist feels, a very infantile, erotic feeling of being in love with myself. A couple shots of bourbon took care of that. If you ever get one, don't flush it down the toilet. It'll kool-aid the water system."

They passed a side street where a long procession of elderly people in wheelchairs were being pushed toward some distant, unseen destination. They were oddly quiet, considering all the surrounding noise.

"Where are they going?" Jason asked.

"I don't know," Phil said.

Jason stopped and watched. "What is this? Where are they going?"

"I don't know where they go, Jason. Nobody asks. "They just go . . . down the street."

"Who are they?"

"They used to be on Medicaid. When that ended the nursing homes couldn't afford to keep them. Every Saturday morning they parked a few out front on the sidewalks. If they weren't picked up they were bussed to churches around the area. Some hired people wheeled them into the morning services and ran. When the service was over they'd be left sitting there. They'd ask them who they came with but they couldn't remember. That really pissed off the Evangelicals. *Are there no workhouses? Are there no poor farms?* They were hell-bent on ending Medicaid but never thought it through. They took them to Human Societies and if nobody adopted them they were brought here. The first ones that were discharged are all gone now, down that street. Most of these here now finally ran out of money for care. I don't know where they all go. Maybe some big shelter. Nobody asks, nobody tells."

"Let's find out." Jason started toward the line. "Come on! I want to know where they go."

"Not now, Jason. The marchers are coming."

"Who?"

"The Banana army. We have to get off the street."

Jason stopped and listened. The sound of a marching cadence grew louder. Twine street quickly cleared of traffic. Pedestrians scattered and disappeared behind storefronts. Jason was able to see them then, a military parade of some sort, heavily-armed marchers wearing orange sashes goose-stepping in Nazi-fashion up the street. He froze.

"Come on, Jason!"

Jason stood and stared. It sounded like a massive chopping machine moving up the street. Phil grabbed his arm and pulled him into the shadows. "They'll be past us in a minute."

Jason could feel the pounding vibrations in his heart. A dog urinated in the street in front of them and ran off.

"This is a practice regimen," Phil said. "The high kick is very difficult, but Trump demands it. That's why their arms are linked, so they won't fall down."

Here and there someone lost step or stumbled when a hip gave out. One comrade in the last row kept kicking the soldier in front of him. "Sorry," he kept saying. "Sorry." When his boot again made contact with the pants in front of him, the soldier turned around and shot the kicker. He fell to the side and the parade marched on.

"Ohmygod," Jason said. "That's Gordon Teasley! Remember I told you about him? My

73

downstairs neighbor?" He ran over and knelt next to the bleeding man.

"Is that you, Jason?" Gordon gasped.

"Yeah, I'm here, Gordon."

"Am I hit bad? Everything's getting cloudy. Am I gonna die?"

"No. It just grazed your ankle. I'll call nine-one-one. Shit! I can't do that! Trump ended it. He said the swamp would drain faster."

"Don't worry about it. Somebody'll come for me. They need me." He pulled the orange scarf from around his waist. "Here, wrap this around it."

"I don't understand any of this, Gordon. Can you lift your foot a little? I don't get why you did it. Why'd you join them? You coulda had class. You coulda been a contender. You coulda been somebody."

"I loved that movie. What was it, The Godfather?"

"On the Waterfront."

"Yeah, that's right. But you're wrong about me, Jason. I was never a contender for anything. I flipped burgers. I was nothing until Trump made me a Banana."

"A marching Banana."

"Better than you. What do *you* have? You guys lost. You got the fear. We got the respect. You answer to us, now." His eyes narrowed. "What are you doing here, anyway?"

"Visiting."

"Visiting who? You don't know nobody around here. You're one of them fucking resisters. I've heard you arguing with your girlfriend—oh boo-hoo civil-rights, human-rights, health-rights, fairy-rights, bitch-rights. Bunch of bleeding heart democrap losers. You're probably one of . . . holy shit, you're one of them Muscles, aren't you?"

"What? No. I never heard of them."

"Bullshit. You're one of them Muscles. That's your car back there. I thought I recognized it."

"I just came down to watch the parade. You need to calm down, Gordon. You're starting to pump blood." Jason pressed down on an imaginary gusher.

"Pump?"

"Your heart's beating fast. It's really pumping it out, man. It's starting to run down the street. I think you're down a quart. No, don't look. It'll just pump harder." He dabbed a trickle of blood.

"Oh god, I'm going to die!"

"You don't look well, Gordon. You're turning gray and pasty. Wait here. I'll go look for help."

Gordon closed his eyes and waited for death. Jason joined Phil on the sidewalk where a small group stood watching.

"That guy over there needs a Band-aid," Jason told them. "Wouldn't hurt to score a point with him." He jerked his head at Phil, indicating *let's go,* and they continued on up the street.

"Is he hurt bad?" Phil asked.

"Not bad enough. He'll be goose-stepping with a limp for a while."

"Still hungry?"

"Not so much. Damn, that was bad back there. What's a Muscle? Gordon accused me of being a Muscle."

"I'll tell you about it when we get back to the office. It's dangerous talk out here."

From somewhere close by, the mournful saxophone poured out the melancholy, never-ending tune. "Who is that?" Jason asked. "It was playing when I got here."

Phil stopped abruptly and looked up at an open third-story window. "Herman!" he called.

The music stopped. "Yeah?" a sad voice said.

"Go to bed!"

"Okay, Phil." The saxophone fell silent.

"That's cool, he listens to you like that," Jason said.

"Funny thing is, I've never met the guy."

"Where are we eating?" Jason could smell the options—grease, garlic, soy sauce, mingling with Lysol and urine fumes in a thick invisible vapor.

"The Acid Reflux. It's right up here."

"Are you kidding?"

"No. Great food, fantastic Reubens."

The Acid Reflux was in the middle of the next block, next to the HOT L; so-called, Phil explained,

76

ever since the rusted E fell out of the overhead HOTEL sign. Five dollars bought a chicken wire cubicle, a dirty bed and bug spray, as much as you needed.

A man wearing an orange sash stood outside the front door of the restaurant.

"Remember what I said," Phil muttered.

Jason held up his wrist, then dropped it tiredly without making eye contact.

"Ronald." Phil nodded to the man. "How's it going?"

The man shrugged and waved them past. Decent smells poured out from the restaurant when Phil opened the door. A sign reading BBB hung in the window.

"Are they kidding?" Jason said. "Better Business Bureau?"

"Bread and broth for a buck," Phil replied.

It wasn't bad inside, an oblong room with a long counter down the right side, in front of a narrow window that looked into a steamy kitchen where two cooks in colored bandanas bustled about. Rusted chrome and Formica tables covered the rest of the linoleum floor on back to a red neon *Restrooms* sign. It was busy and actually looked clean. Several homeless filled the counter stools, hunched over their BBB. Phil aimed for a table against the wall, halfway down the left side. "Face in or out," he asked.

"Doesn't matter," Jason said. Phil took the chair facing the wall. A hairy man in baggy tan pants and a tight polyester shirt hugging a sagging mass of belly ambled over with two menus. He nodded at Phil, gave Jason a tired look devoid of interest, and ambled away. "Wave when you're ready," he muttered.

The choices were mostly sandwiches, all grilled, all served with fries and dill pickles.

"I guess I'll have the Reuben," Jason said, "if you think it's good."

Phil turned and held up his hand, indicated two fingers and settled back.

"Do you mind if I ask a personal question?" Jason asked.

"I don't know. Ask it and we'll find out."

"Why do you have your office in the worst part of town? I mean, it was dangerous even before Trump. Aren't you nervous one of your clients will get robbed or shot or something?"

"We can get shot anywhere now, Jason. I don't know that one place is any safer than another anymore."

"With your money you can set up anywhere."

"No. That ship sailed. I have to pay protection money now."

"You can't leave?"

"Yeah, I can leave, but I decided I could accomplish more here. I want my clients out of their comfort zones. Someplace they have to stick their heads and necks out and grow a pair."

"I have a pair."

"But you don't own them. I'm not carpeting your rut, Jason. Look around. You'll learn something."

"Oh I have. I feel completely safe from ISIS here." He tapped his fingers on the tabletop.

"Are you nervous?" Phil asked.

"Not especially. I was just thinking, thirty-four years old and a bachelor's degree in physics and this is where my life is."

"Where do you wish it was?"

"On a yacht. I'd like to travel all over the world, sail the high seas, except near Somalia, or Nigeria, or Kenya, or Indonesia, or Tanzania, or Peru, or Bangladesh, or Thailand, or Vietnam, or the Philippines, or Malaysia, or Ecuador, or Guatemala, or Venezuela. Too many pirates. I could carry missile launchers and water hoses, but one of them could stop working and I would never get any sleep worrying about it. I might as well just stay home and wait for a nuclear warhead to hit my house."

The waiter, or owner, or whatever he was, brought two glasses of ice water. "Your order's coming up," he said. He was carrying a roll of paper towels under his arm. He set it down in the middle of the table and shuffled off.

Phil pulled his chair forward, smiling as he watched the waiter return carrying two paper-lined plastic baskets. "Okay," he said. "Get ready. This is great stuff!" He rubbed his hands together in anticipation of the savory food set before them.

The sandwiches were at least five inches thick; mountains of shaved corned beef, heaps of sauerkraut, gobs of rich dressing wrapped in butter-grilled rye bread and slices of melted Swiss.

Jason worked a giant bite into his mouth. "Oh I *gaw*," he groaned, warm cheese and dressing oozing out. "I sound like Amy." They said nothing for five minutes, until half their sandwiches were consumed.

Jason wiped his greasy fingers on a paper towel. "I need a cigarette," he said. He ate a fry. "What kind of dressing is that?"

"Russian. What else?"

Jason sat back and thought a moment. "Did you know Russia has built a huge underground city in the Ural Mountains? The Yamantou Mountain Complex. They have large train tracks running in and out of it, enormous caves, tens of thousands of workers, warehouses with enough provisions—food, water, clothes—to last for months."

"No, I hadn't heard that. This Reuben is unbelievable, isn't it? I could—"

"It's been built to resist direct nuclear hits. Even if their cities are destroyed the military and political bigwigs, their nuclear command center, would survive. It'll hold sixty-thousand people. They've spent billions upgrading. The air filtration system is designed to withstand even chemical and biological attacks."

"Why don't we finish eating and then—"

"One of their defected intelligence officers, even our own people, have said that the only potential use for this site is post-nuclear survival. It is the largest nuclear-secure project in the world."

"Oh yeah?"

"They think the Russians have two-hundred more deep underground sites around the country, smaller versions for the same purpose. Surviving nuclear war."

Jason stared at Phil, waiting for some reaction, any reaction, to this deeply disturbing information. Phil continued eating, undisturbed. "You're not getting it," Jason said.

"I'm listening, Jason. I'm just waiting for your point."

"You disappoint me, Phil. The point's pretty friggin' obvious." He leaned forward, waiting until Phil finished chewing. "The point is, where's our Yamantou?"

Phil thought. "Trump probably has one."

"I'm sure he does. *Trumptou: The Greatest Hole on Earth.* How come he's not promising to build one for the rest of us?"

81

Phil shrugged."

"I'll tell you why. Because he'd only let whites in. All the elite would pay millions but he'd only allow enough worker ants to keep it running. He's not planning anything for the peasants."

"We have bunkers."

"Of course. For the regime. The rest of us can buy missile silos. Two million cash for a fixer-upper. It's a seller's market. Kushner's handling it. Ivanka's dividing them into condos."

Phil squirted ketchup into his basket and dunked three fries. "Would you live in one?"

"No." Jason picked up his sandwich. "This is cold. Do you think they'd reheat it?"

"I doubt it."

"Could you ask?"

"You can ask." Phil looked around, then raised his arm. Jason heard the familiar shuffling headed toward the table. Phil pointed to Jason.

"Yeah?" the man said.

"Could you reheat this sandwich for me?"

"Sure."

"That would be great." Jason started to hand over the basket.

"I don't need the basket. How long do you want it in my armpit?"

"What?"

"I recommend a minute, to steam it clear through. Keep the meat moist."

82

"Yeah, okay, I get it. Never mind. Thanks anyway."

"Sure you don't need a doily?"

"Did I ask for one?"

The man gave Phil a flat look and left the check. "You got a testy one this time." He removed something from his pocket and slid it across the table to Jason.

"What's this?" Jason turned it over. "A picture of Mike Pence?" He glowered at the phony grin. "Makes me sick looking at it. You want me to throw up my lunch?"

The man smirked. Jason's answer seemed to please him. "Keep it. It'll come in handy when you need it."

Jason slid it into a back pocket. "Weird."

"Not really. How does it make you feel?"

"Pissed. Frustrated."

"Motivated?"

"Oh yeah."

"Good. That's good, Jason. Take it out once in a while. It's a good reminder that this thing that happened, Trump's coronation, it's not just about Trump. We have a whole nest of Complicits to clean out."

"We?"

"Sure. Did you think you were in this thing alone? You're officially one of us, now."

"One of who?" Jason stared at him. "Are you

part of some underground movement? Is it what Gordon was talking about, the Muscles?"

"I'd rather wait till we got back to the office to talk about it. The Bananas don't all wear sashes, okay?"

"Right. Okay."

"So . . . getting back to where we were—why not?"

"Why not what?"

"Wouldn't you live in a missile silo?"

"Would you?"

"No. But I didn't ruin my lunch worrying about it."

"I can't breathe recycled air for very long. I can hardly make it through a movie. I have to breathe through my hand. It's subtle. Amy hasn't noticed. I just sit there, like this." He held his elbow in one hand and cupped a hand loosely over his mouth. "It just looks like I'm really into the movie. I put a little mint between my fingers and lick it now and then to keep the scent coming."

Phil quirked his brows and looked keenly at him. "Really, Jason?"

"Absolutely. You don't know where the air's been, who's coughed in it or farted in it. Did you know you can see farts in cold weather? It's true. The same way you can see warm breath. It trails after you too, man. They're hard to walk away from."

84

"Do you know why farts smell?" Phil asked. "So deaf people can enjoy them, too."

They both laughed, loud enough for a few heads to glance in their direction.

"But no," Jason said. "I could never live in a tube. I have claustrophobia. I got caught in a tight pullover once, trying to take it off. It was like being in a straitjacket. I couldn't text for help. I couldn't move my arms up or down. I started to sweat and have a panic attack. I tried to grab it with my teeth. I rolled around on the floor trying to catch it on something. I finally snagged it on a door stop. It looked like I was trying to fuck the wall. If Amy had come home and found me like that, that would have been it. Finished! Adios, wall fucker!"

Phil laughed, so loudly everyone in the room turned to look at their table. Jason shrank in his seat but they weren't looking at him. Tears filled Phil's eyes. He leaned forward with his elbows on the table and covered his face with both hands. He giggled another full minute.

Phil finally sat back, working to compose himself. "Okay, sorry." He sniffed and swallowed. "Say something serious."

"That was serious. This has me seriously worried. I don't think you're taking my case seriously."

"I am, Jason, I am. Believe me." He ripped off a paper towel and wiped his mouth. "I'm sorry. Let's get this back on track. If you could never live in a missile silo —"

"Or an underground cave."

"Or there, why do you care whether we have a Yamantou?"

"Well, thank you. Apparently, I don't impress you as the kind of person who gives a shit about my fellow man . . . fellow country-people. What about Amy? What about all the Ones fighting this? Even if there isn't a nuclear holocaust, when the Mexicans escape back across the border and the economy collapses there's going to be complete chaos and starvation. At the very least I should be stockpiling more food but I'm running out of places to hide it. The first place marauders will look is under my bed. "I could create a diversion, set something on fire. Amy has some diet food in the cupboard, but then what? I've thought about a safe deposit box but the banks would probably be looted, or charge horrible fees. Paper money would be worthless. What happens when I run out of gold fillings?"

"Are you going to eat that?" Phil nodded toward the half-eaten sandwich.

"No. The cheese is rubbery."

"It wasn't." Phil wrapped it in a paper towel.

"It is now."

"Not for long." Phil put a few bills on the table and stood to leave.

86

"The canned foods already have expiration dates," Jason said, following him out the door, "and I rotate frequently so I won't get food poisoning. But what about fruit and vegetables? I could just write "soon" on those. Thank god I bought before the tariff wars. Prunes are forty-dollars a pound. I should hurry and buy freeze-dried. They're supposed to have a *just-picked* taste for up to fifteen years. The pouches are nitrogen flushed. I could buy a two-year entree plan but where would I hide the toilet paper? And that's not even including breakfast food. I need to prepare for the most important meal of the day. And the Ghirardelli chocolate bucket. Is a hundred and sixty servings enough?"

A passing hooptie blared its horn and Phil waved. Jason didn't hear it.

"The worst thing, though, is the thought of hunting for food. I don't think I could shoot something more scared than I am. Some of them could be fatty. Possums look lean, from what I've seen on the highway. Why aren't more chickens crossing the road? Would I need a hunting license if I used my car? What am I saying? I could never do it. I'd see that deer-in-the-headlights look and drive my car up a tree. It would go on my CLUE report. Then what? I don't have anarchy insurance."

They stopped while Phil handed the half-eaten sandwich to a homeless man sitting against the building. A large bonfire was burning in the middle of the street. People were throwing in Trump propaganda and running before the Bananas caught them.

"Are you listening to me?" Jason said. He stood and watched Phil continue walking toward the office.

"Every word."

"None of this bothers you?" He jogged to catch up.

"Some of it. I'm working on the percentages." He stopped outside the stairwell door. Another horn quickly blared.

Jason turned to see an old red pickup parked just up the street. The driver quickly hunkered low in the seat. Something registered in the back of his mind but didn't connect. "What percentages?" he asked.

"You reminded me, in that smart-ass tone I've come to love, that I'm a detective and I should be able to spot your horseshit."

"I don't think any horseshit has entered the conversation."

"So I've been keeping track of it. You want the breakdown? Sixty percent of everything out of your mouth is legitimate. Thirty percent is shtick. Ten percent is pure horseshit. That's a compliment, Jason. It's much better to be a horse-shitter than a bull-shitter."

"What's the difference?"

88

"Purely subjective. To me, in my opinion, horseshit is ridiculous, it's harmless nonsense. Bullshit is a deliberate lie. Some people hold the opposite view. This is mine."

"Thirty percent is shtick?"

"On average. Sometimes it's one-hundred percent. It's how you've kept a handle on the takeover. Comedy is your Ativan. Except it's not doing the job anymore. We're getting there, Jason. Hang in there. Only nineteen more hours to go."

"If I live that long. I feel a bullet coming on."

They glanced again at the pickup parked across the street as Phil opened the door. Drake stepped out as they stepped in.

"Thanks, Drake," Phil said.

Jason dodged a bird dropping halfway up the stairs.

The spider was gone.

—5—

The 1985 faded red Chevy pickup circled the block three times, dodging bonfires before rejoining the smelly caravan of junkers cruising Twine Street. It was the only oil-burner not blasting rap music, but it blended anyway, adding its own clanks, rumbles and coughs to a cacophony of raucous noise.

This trip around it stopped alongside an empty parking space in front of Cubic Hair, hopefully a beauty parlor business. It paused a moment, then began the arduous task of backing and forwarding, gaining by jerks and squeals and oinks until the square-bodied truck was aligned with the curb, tight between an old Ford and something older and green. The driver turned off the ignition. The engine rumbled, coughed and died. Not bad, she thought. Not bad at all.

Amy McFine slouched down in the driver's seat of her father's decrepit truck, her long hair tucked beneath a Mariners baseball cap. Concealed behind dark glasses, she stared at the light blue Prius parked across the street. She wore a high-collared hunting jacket and matching pants, camouflage colors so she'd look more earthy in the worst part of town. The doors were locked but she double checked anyway. The windows were obscured with rain-splattered dust. She withdrew an iPhone from a jacket pocket and tapped a speed dial number.

"He did it," she whispered hoarsely. "He's here. His car's parked across the street. He kept the appointment."

"Good," a female replied. "Now get out of there."

"It's okay. I'm safe. It's really loud here."

"Then why are you whispering?"

"I don't know. I feel like I'm hiding. I'm not scared, though. I thought I'd be scared but I'm not."

"Being scared has nothing to do with it. Most people who are attacked aren't scared because they don't know they're going to be attacked until they're attacked. You don't know who's watching you right now."

Amy checked the mirrors. "No one's looking at me. People are just wandering around. There's a bonfire in the street and people are throwing stuff in it and running."

"Any orange scarves?"

"I saw a couple on another street. I don't see any right now. There's a few small groups on the corners."

"Also known as gangs."

"Paying no attention to me, just talking to each other."

"You are out of your mind, do you know that? I don't understand why you're doing this."

"Because I had to know. It's better than wondering all day and night if he did it."

"What difference does it make now? You broke up."

Amy paused. "Yeah," she said weakly.

"Oh, that was believable. You changed your mind again? Tell me you haven't changed your mind again."

"I don't know. I'm confused."

"He's not going to change."

"I don't know if I want him to change."

"What?! Oh god, you've gone melancholy."

"No, I just mean that . . . I don't know. Other than the part that makes me sick—"

"A huge part."

"Okay, maybe, but I really love him. I can't help it. He's funny. He can be so romantic. Did I tell you about the potatoes? He's thoughtful, he worries about me—"

"He's obsessive, he drives you crazy, he never shuts up, he stores grain in his closet—"

"But he was right. Everything he said would happen is happening. I didn't want to believe it and he wouldn't shut up about it, but he wouldn't do anything about it but bitch, so yes! It drove me crazy! I warned him so many times!"

"Do you need to use the bathroom?" He was shaving, she was wearing a short chenille robe, standing with her back against the bathroom door, hugging her arms, watching him.

"No," she said tiredly.

"Something wrong?"

"Nothing more than usual."

"Okay." He waited a moment, then started shaving again.

"You're AWOL from this relationship, Jason."

"I—"

"No, let me finish, it's different this time. I want you to go see Phil Magnum."

"Okay, I'm ready to do that. I'll look up his address when I'm done shaving."

"It's on Twine Street."

He froze. "That's in Donald's Inferno. You seriously want me to go into Donald's Inferno?"

"It's only a one-day session, just twenty-four hours."

"Just? You know how many people die there in twenty-four hours?"

"No. Do you?"

"It's a lot, at least one an hour. I heard they're down to twenty-three residents now. My odds getting out alive would not be good, Amy."

"You have a full body armor suit in the closet, next to your face plate."

"You're serious," he said. She clearly was. "Let me finish shaving, then we can talk."

"No more talk. Either you'll go or you won't. I can't deal with your rants anymore about Trump and the Complicits and the takeover. You don't think I'm scared? I know what they've done is terrible. I know it's not our country anymore, but we don't have a life together anymore, either. You're so consumed with it you don't have time for me. We don't talk about any of the normal things couples talk about when they live together."

Oh shit, he thought. Here we go.

"Do you ever think about us getting married someday? Do you want to have kids? Would you ever like to buy a house? These are just normal questions about our future, Jason. Do we even have a future? I don't know what kind of romance we have anymore."

"Romance is hard even when the world isn't going crazy. These aren't normal times . . ."

"Romance isn't hard, Jason. Romance just is."

"Romance just IS if you're a woman. All the woman has to do is put on a nightie. For a guy it's a colossal pain in the ass because when you say you want to talk about "romance," that means there's going to be a very stressful conversation. We would rather nail our fucking tongues to a fucking tree than have that fucking conversation, Amy!"

She just stared at him. He hung his head. His shoulders slumped. "I'm sorry. I didn't mean that. I'll see Magnum. I guess I can take a day off work and get it over with." She spun around and grabbed the doorknob. "Wait a minute! Where are you going?"

"A long, long way from here. Go nail your tongue to a tree."

"I said I'd go. I want to go. I'm just not awake yet, that's all. Give me Magnum's number. Where is it, in your pocket? On the desk? I'll call this morning. Do you have a pencil? Let me get a pencil and a piece of toilet paper and I'll make a list of everything you want me to do, the salient points. I'll put together a PowerPoint presentation for him so it won't take all day. We can go out to dinner afterward. I'm feeling really empowered now, Amy. I'm ready to take charge."

She stood staring at him, waiting to hear more.

"I understand why you think I'm AWOL. Well, not completely, but ballpark I hear you. Can we nail this down? Can we do that?" He turned off the razor. "I'm just saying, if I understood the rules, maybe I wouldn't have to see Magnum. I would just promise to follow the rules from now on."

"There aren't any rules."

"Of course there are. That's why we're having this argument. I am guilty of more don'ts than do's so let's fine-tune this."

She shrugged. "Okay."

"When is my talking about what's going on in Trumpssia, too much? Less than an hour after dessert? Within fifteen minutes of sex? Is a half hour before, but not during, dinner okay? On the way going somewhere but not coming back? Never on Friday and Sunday night? How about if two-thirds of the conversation is about us and one-third is serious stuff."

"We're not serious?"

"You have to cut me some slack here, Amy. I don't keep a thesaurus next to the toilet."

"Are you done?"

"Yes. Because the great thing about this argument is that it's only going to take half the time, since only half of this relationship is the problem."

She tilted her head, narrowed her eyes. "What does that mean?"

"It means I'm the one who's annoying and you're perfect."

"That's a rotten thing to say. I don't deserve that."

He threw up his hands. "I don't believe this. I'm in trouble here because I said you're perfect?"

"Yes. It sounds like you're giving me a compliment but you're not. You're shifting the

96

blame on me, Jason. I'm all good and you're all bad, boo-hoo. And by the way, I hate it that you think I'm perfect. I'm always afraid I'll say the wrong thing and I'll deflate in your eyes, or the light will dim or whatever will happen when you find out I'm not the perfect person you think I am."

He stared at her. Several seconds passed. She shifted uneasily. Her brows furrowed. "What!" she snapped. "What does that look mean?"

"I know that you don't always flush after you pee. I know that sometimes you only wash your bangs so it looks like you took a shower when you don't have time. I know you order crap from HSN you don't need because it only costs five easy payments. I know you think NAFTA is a country in Africa. You will never deflate in my eyes, Amy, because I will never understand how I got so lucky to have someone I love so much standing in front of my eyes in the first place."

She twisted her mouth. "Is that it?"

"Yes."

Her eyes teared. "You make me sick, Jason."

"I know. I'm sorry. Can I take your temperature?"

Her friend sighed heavily. "Look Amy, Jason is one of my best friends. I'd date him myself if he was a woman and had tape over his mouth. But nobody, *nobody*, could live with the way he is."

"But he's here. He did it."

"He's there now but you don't know if anything's going to change. Go home before somebody sees you're a woman sitting there alone. Go home and give it a few weeks and see if he's any different."

"Yes. You're right."

"Are you putting the key in the ignition?"

"It's already . . .ohmygod!"

"What! *What?!*"

"There he is! Jason. I see him. He's coming up the street, not on my side, the other side. He's talking to some man in a suit. It must be Magnum. Jason's talking a lot, flailing his arms. The man is kind of ignoring him."

"Yeah, that's definitely Jason. What does the other guy look like? Phil Magnum."

"I can't see him very well from here. Tall, slim, sharp dresser, wearing a hat, one of those kinds detectives wear. He just stopped and handed something to somebody sitting on the sidewalk. Here they come again. Jason's running to catch up." She leaned forward to get a better look through the murky windshield. The horn abruptly blared and she flew backward and crouched down in the seat.

"Was that your horn? Amy! Was that your horn?"

"Yes!" she whispered. "I accidentally hit it." She peered over the top of the steering wheel. "Phil Magnum's looking at me right now!"

"Is Jason looking?"

"Yes."

"Would he recognize the truck?"

"I don't think so. He's not looking anymore. He's busy talking."

"Good old Jason. Is Magnum still looking?"

"Yes. No. He's talking to Jason. Still talking. They're going into the building now. They're looking at me again! Okay, they're gone."

"Now you get yourself gone! I mean it, Amy."

"I will. I need to calm down a minute. I'll call you when I get to work."

"Call me as soon as you're out of there."

"I will. I promise." She closed her eyes and waited until the shivering subsided and her breathing slowed. She closed her eyes and waited until the shivering subsided and her breathing slowed. None of this seemed real. It was as though she was outside the window, looking in at herself. After several minutes she slid back up in the seat and stared at Jason's car. Thank God he didn't recognize the truck. She took a deep breath. Hopefully the worst was over. There was a blast in the distance, like an explosion. A stream of black smoke began to curl into the sky beyond the rooftops.

She saw the shadow first, then a specter, tall, brooding. It appeared suddenly next to the driver's door. It tapped on the glass. It was a large man in dark clothes, his scruffy face inches from the window.

Amy swallowed and lowered her voice. "Get lost," she growled. "This is a stakeout."

"Do you have any change?" he asked.

"I don't know. Just a minute." Amy felt around her pockets. "I don't have any change. Is a dollar okay?"

"Yeah. I'll make it work."

Amy cranked the window down a quarter inch, inserted the bill and fed it through. It was a ten. Damn. Okay. Whatever.

He reached up and took it. "Thanks. I appreciate it."

"You're welcome."

He hesitated a moment. "You need to lock your door."

"It is locked."

"No. I had an old truck like this. The knob's down but it's not down into the lock. You need to give it a stronger push."

She turned sideways and pressed down hard on the button. There was resistance.

"Whack it with your fist."

She did. It thumped into locked position. "Thanks," she said.

"You're welcome. Good luck with your stakeout."

She watched him amble up the street, leaned forward to turn the ignition, then froze. The door to Magnum's building suddenly burst open. Out stormed Jason, angry eyes fixed on her as he strode quickly across the street.

—6—

Open the door," Jason said. "Open the fucking door!"

Amy pulled hard on the passenger door lock. "I'm trying!"

The second it released he was inside the truck, slamming and locking the door. "What are you doing here?"

"I . . .I just came to see if you came. I've only been here a minute. I'll go now."

"Do you know how stupid this is? Do you have any fucking idea how dangerous it is here?"

"Yes."

"No, you don't. You hear those blasts? Magnum told me they're shoulder-fired missiles. They're practicing. You see those places where the roofs have been blown out? They can't hit the fucking sky half the time. We're in the pandemonium time zone now, noon till nine. God-dammit, Amy! What were you thinking?"

"Then let's go. You come with me. I didn't know it was going to be like this."

"I'm not running now. You wanted me to do this and I'm going to do it. I could deal with the *'whiner'* part, what you called me, but I'm not *'impotent.'"* She opened her mouth to speak but he cut her off. "I want to do this, whether we broke up or not. Have we?"

"I don't know. I think so."

"Okay, well, *hasta la vista*, baby. I can take care of myself. I have survival skills you wouldn't believe. I've been places rats are scared to go. If you don't hear from me by noon tomorrow, *no problem*o. I'll probably just be in surgery. Get out of here now, move someplace warm while you still can. Take a water purifier with you. And a hazmat suit. It's in the hall closet."

She was staring up the street. "Who are they?"

Jason stared at the front row of marchers wearing orange sashes less than a block away. "Shit! Get down! Can you get under the wheel?"

"Not all of me. I have an ass, you know." They crouched down low and tight. "Who are they?" The sound of pounding boots grew closer.

"Bananas. They came through here an hour ago. They'll be past in a minute."

"Are we illegal or something? Aren't we allowed on the street?"

"They look for trouble. And you're gorgeous, so, you know. And one of them hates me, now."

103

"What are they singing? It reminds me of that army marching into the witch's castle in the Wizard of Oz. Did you ever wonder what they were saying? It sounded like '*Or-E-o, HO-Hum*', to me."

They listened to the approaching cadence. "It's what they sing when they deliver Trump's dinner— '*Bay-CON cheese, MAY-o.*'"

"Oh god, they're right next to us!" She reached over and squeezed his hand. "What if they look in the window?"

"Get on top of me. They'll watch but won't interrupt."

"I don't know how you can joke. This is a nightmare. I should have listened to you. I should have believed you. I'm so sorry, Jason. I never thought it could happen. I always thought there were powerful people out there with millions of dollars and they'd never let this happen. Didn't you think they would stop this? Even when he was putting the crown on his head I thought somebody would step forward and stop it." She started to cry. "Now our country's gone! I should have done something! I should have prayed more!"

"Voting might have helped."

"That's right," she cried. "Blame me. It's all my fault."

"Could you keep your sobbing down to a dull wail? Here, look at this." He pulled a photograph from his back pocket. She stared, then grimaced. "Pence? Put it away! I can't stand that toady grin."

"Great rallying tool, isn't it? Your reaction was like mine. It gives me this visceral urge to squeeze his face into a jelly jar. He thinks he's the Chosen One. When Trump's gone he'll mount his high horse and the Tombs and Vipers will ride with him. They believe God ordained all this. Pious Pence in his white helmet is just biding his time, waiting to ascend. Have you looked at his eyes?"

"Not the doll's eyes speech again."

"They're worse. Pence looks half asleep but he's scrutinizing, calculating his rise to power. Every time Trump fucks up he turns into the Cheshire cat. He's just an innocent bystander. He's out of the loop, nobody tells him anything, he wasn't there, he was someplace else—and he slowly disappears and all that's left is that creepy grin."

"Where'd you get the picture?"

"They're handed out down here. I heard something about a group called the Muscles. I haven't found out much about them yet."

A hard knock on the window jolted them wide-eyed. Phil frowned down at them. "They're gone. You're Amy? Nice to meet you. Now get the hell out of here." Jason helped pull her back up into the seat.

"Don't go down Twine, either way," Phil told her. "Back up the truck and take that street, go three blocks and take a right on Port. Don't stop for anything. Not *anything*, you hear me? All the red lights are torn down so just keep going." He turned back across the street.

"Come with me, Jason," Amy pleaded. "You've proved enough. Please!"

"Nah." He got out and slapped the hood. "Get going."

"Please don't die, Jason. I'll never forgive myself if you die."

"I won't tell you, then." He backed away and waved. The old truck shuddered and coughed and creaked backward, then turned onto the side street and disappeared. A brawl broke out on the corner close to the Acid Reflux. Further down the block a roof exploded. Black smoke and ashes filtered down into the street. Jason jogged back to the office.

"She's very pretty," Phil said.

"We're still broke up. I asked her. Love is so fickle. One little mistake and I'm another broken body on the trash-heap of discarded, misunderstood lovers."

"She came down here. She was worried about you."

"She felt guilty. If I die she doesn't want it on her conscience."

"You're being colossally unfair, Jason."

"What do I care if I'm fair? The next missile could come right through that window. That's not fair, either. Nothing's fair anymore." He glanced at his watch. "We need to kick this up a notch. You've only got nineteen and a half hours left to debug me and I'm not feeling it." A siren suddenly blared and screamed past the office and down the street. "Do you think Amy's okay?"

"She's fine. The route I gave her is pretty safe this time of day."

"So, what are the Muscles?"

"An underground movement, the *Make the United States Constitution Legal Eagles*. After Trump replaced the Constitution with his Dictum, the group grew pretty fast. We're up to several million patriots now. Trump banned copies of the Constitution, but he couldn't burn them all."

"What happened to the original?"

"We got it out of the National Archives before the takeover, that and the Bill of Rights and the Declaration of Independence. They're safe."

"Are you one of the organizers?"

"No. It was already on a roll before Louie clued me in on it."

"Louie?"

"Your friendly waiter."

"You're kidding. That guy?"

Phil raised his brows. "What's your point?"

Jason shrugged. "He doesn't look like a . . . like a rebel, I guess."

"How are they supposed to look, like Schwarzenegger?"

"Yeah okay, it was a dumb reaction."

"That's part of your problem, Jason. You're a judgmental guy. It's not even buried that deep."

"That's not true. I'm not judgmental . . ."

Phil held up his hand. "I heard that speech a few hours ago. What was it you said, something like, you frequently offend people, but in a completely open, honest way. You can't help it if people are too stupid to see it."

Jason sank back and closed his eyes. "Okay. You win. Point for you."

Phil snorted a laugh. "So that's how you play it? Points?"

"No! Jesus! Whose side are you on?"

"Mine. That's why you're here. Your side's losing."

"I wish now I'd finished taking self-defense lessons," Jason grumbled. "Martial arts, something to release the pressure."

"How would that change anything?"

"All the anger wouldn't build up, you know, make me such a prick, I guess what you're saying. It might have helped my bedroom moves, too—synergy, the perfect combination of horniness and skill . . . what's that noise?"

Drake was standing outside, tapping on the glass.

Phil removed a plastic bag from the desk and shoved open the window. A flow of acrid air and unnerving street noise poured in. He sprinkled a handful of seed on the ledge. "Sorry I'm late, Drake. We have a very interesting client today." Phil closed the window and turned on the box fan. "So, you started taking self-defense lessons because why?"

"Bruce Lee. Enter the Dragon. Carry the girl into the bedroom wearing just a black belt. *He-e-e YAH! Who-who-who-HA! Hi-YAH! E-e-e-YUH!* Oh yeah, swift, with power."

"How far did you get?"

"Somewhere between meditate, warm-up and stretch, to kicks, strikes and blocks. It didn't totally make sense. How could I hit someone with my shoes if I was barefoot? The whacking wasn't too bad but what if I was accosted in an alley and I wasn't carrying my bamboo stick? They said I had to learn not to be there when they struck. I thought, why in the hell would I have to learn anything else if I knew that? They said I cried too much. They said as long as I insisted on being a complete yin I could never find my yang. I think I'm better suited to gouging, poking and scratching. I need to learn some techniques that don't hurt, me I mean, to protect myself."

"From what?"

Jason shot him an incredulous look. "Are you kidding me? More than fourteen thousand people are murdered in this country every year. That was even before Trumpssia. It's probably double that, now. Come on, Phil. You listen to bootleg news. How could you ask me something so stupid?"

"Okay, you're right. It was stupidly put. What I meant was, is there any one thing in particular that makes you feel especially threatened?"

"Yes. Violent death. Death by everything the Banana bunch uses —handguns, knives, corkscrews, hammers, head-butts, clubs, hatchets, bottles, bats, fire, needles, pliers, assault rifles, ropes, shotguns, other guns. I should get a gun. I don't want a gun. Almost everyone has one now. Hundreds of millions of guns out there, not counting the military. We are the best-armed civilians in the world, except me; eighty-nine firearms for every hundred people."

"That doesn't mean eighty-nine people out of a hundred have a gun. Some people have a lot of guns. A lot of people don't have any. Does Amy have a gun?"

"No."

"Do her parents?"

"Yes. They keep it in a safe. That's where I'd keep it. Under my bed, behind the canned goods."

"So, if you woke up in the middle of the night and heard a noise, you'd open the safe and get your gun and go downstairs?"

"Or, I'd crawl on my belly to the bedroom door and lock it, then call nine-one-one and try not to scream too loud—shit! I keep forgetting Trump cut nine-one-one. I guess I'd probably crawl over to the bed and get the gun out of the safe, then make a little noise so they'd hear I was awake and hopefully leave, then I'd sit in a corner facing the door and wait."

"What if they didn't leave? What if you heard them coming up the stairs? What if you saw the doorknob start to turn?"

Jason thought hard. "Okay, this is bad. If I say, *'Who is it?'* I could have door splinters and an Uzi in my face."

"Or Amy could be in the hall wondering why the door is locked."

"Right. So, I couldn't shoot through the door. Who believed that Pistorius bullshit anyway? This is good, doing a mental trial-run now. So okay, I could say, *'Whoever you are, you should know I have a gun and I know how to use it.'* No, I shouldn't say that last part. I giggle when I'm lying. I would just warn them that I had a gun. Should I say what kind?"

"No."

"Yeah, you're right. Let them think I might have a machine gun or something. Maybe a missile launcher. I'd tell them I had a gun, and I don't have a safe and if I did there's only seven dollars in it. And my credit cards are all maxed out. You know, just keep the conversation going till they decide to rob someplace else. Do you have a gun?"

"Yes."

"Are you wearing it?"

"No."

"Is it here? In the office?"

"Yes."

"Can I see it?"

Phil removed a pistol from a side drawer and slid it halfway across the desk.

"Is it loaded?"

"Yes."

Jason leaned forward, staring hard at it. "What kind is it?"

"Smith & Wesson .357 magnum revolver."

"How many cartridges does it hold?"

"Six rounds."

"Where do you carry it?"

"Almost everywhere."

"No, I mean, on your body."

"I have a belt holster."

"Does it press on your kidney? Mine couldn't stand any more pressure."

"No."

"You need a license for that, right?"

"A concealed weapon license, yes."

Jason leaned in closer. "Have you ever fired it?"

"At a shooting range."

"Ever at a person?"

"No."

"Do you think you could, if you had to?"

"If I had to."

Jason gnawed a knuckle, studying it, thinking. "I could get a Rottweiler. My insurance would go up, though. Most claims are from dog bites. I could just get a dog barking machine. Amy wants to—wanted to—adopt a shelter dog."

"How do you feel about that?"

"Yeah, it would be okay. I'd like a dog." Jason leaned back, looking pale. "Okay, you can put the gun away now." When it was out of sight he said, "See, that's the thing. I don't think I could shoot a gun at anything with body hair."

"I think you'd need to be in that position first to make that decision."

"Will a creep go away if I pretend I don't see him?"

"Doubt it."

"The thing is, I think maybe I could shoot if I absolutely had to, if my life depended on it, but how would I know for sure? I'd have to ask them some questions first. Not a lot of questions. If they're in a hurry it would only take a minute."

"So you could decide whether or not to shoot them."

"Yes. Exactly. I'd whip out my gun and say, like, 'Are you attacking me because you need food?' 'Could we settle this if I buy you dinner?' 'Do you accept gift cards?' 'Are you going to just rob me or do you think you're going to kill me, too?' 'If I give you my wallet, can I have the condom back? It's the first one I ever used.'"

"Not seriously."

"No, but it might defuse the situation. Show them I'm just a regular guy like them, maybe in the market for a gang."

Phil scratched his forehead. "Do you want to go down there on the street tonight and try that? I'll stay up here and cover you."

"Would I get a refund?"

"If I said yes, would you go down there?"

"No. I'm just trying to work this out, have a game plan. It was bad out there even before Trump. Now it's . . . aren't you scared at all?"

"I'm concerned."

"Did you hear that some NRA lobbyists were cited for indecent exposure? They were caught on a park bench, feeling-up their rifles."

Phil chuckled.

"I have to make jokes to handle it. Nice people just . . . gone in a second, watching a concert, sitting in kindergarten, some innocent black kid walking home. This is the Weltschmerz you said, right?"

"Yes."

Jason leaned forward, looking hard at Phil. "That's a piss-poor word for what I'm feeling right now. I can't tell you what I'm feeling. It's so deep I don't know where it goes or what's down there when it gets there. It's pretty bad, pretty ugly, someplace horrible, like looking inside my Aunt Brisky's nostrils, two huge, hairy, black hellholes. I can't joke my way out of there anymore. It's not working. *I'm* not working." He held up both hands, smiling. "But hey, at least pot's legal now. Do you know the difference between a drunk and a stoner at a stop sign? The drunk runs it and the stoner waits for it to turn green."

"You do a lot of pot, Jason?"

"Not much. Do you?"

"Not much." Phil stood and headed for the fridge. "Need a drink?"

"Yeah. Water's okay. So, what's the cure for Weltschmerz? Can you put it in a brownie?"

"You have something better than that, Jason." He cracked the cap off a bottle of orange juice and took several long swallows.

"What do I have that's better?" Jason asked.

Phil sat back down. "You're funny."

"And I just said, that's not working anymore."

"Because you have it parked in the wrong place. Let me tell you something else, first. Having Weltschmerz doesn't feel good, but it says something good about you. You care. If you didn't give a shit what's going on with anybody, anywhere, I would give you your money back and refer you somewhere else."

"Somebody told me once where I could shove my jokes. Is it the same place you're talking about?"

"I'm talking about the big picture."

Jason snorted. "You mean like, *The Divine Plan*? I tried to see that once. Somebody's head was blocking the screen. Do you believe in a divine plan?"

"That's not exactly—"

"I keep asking God, what is my purpose in life? What is your plan for my future? What is my destiny? I never get an answer. One night I climbed out my bedroom window and sat on the roof and I told God I wasn't moving until I got an answer. I sat outside all night, watching the stars, watching the house across the street get burgled.

"After they robbed that place the burglars were coming across the street to hit my house when they saw me and stopped. I waved. They waved back. They got in their getaway U-Haul and took off. I would have lost everything if I hadn't been sitting out there.

"God probably had a good laugh about that. I gave him the point."

—7—

"Are you wishing now you ate all your lunch?" Phil asked.

"Yeah. Are we going to the same place again?"

"Best place around. They fancy things up for dinner."

"I can't wait."

Jason stood aside the window like a shadow and watched the bustling street-hustle while Phil used the bathroom. Where was Amy now, he wondered. Packing up her things? At work? Trying to call him? He was tempted to quickly retrieve his phone from the desk drawer and check for messages.

But maybe Phil wasn't actually going to the bathroom. Maybe this was a test, to see what he would do, test his integrity. He removed a small round pill container attached to his keychain, unscrewed the cap and was removing a dark red capsule when the bathroom door opened. He wouldn't have made it. Phil would have caught him. His heart hammered at the thought.

"What's that?" Phil asked.

"Krill oil. It helps keep my blood platelets from sticking."

"How do you know your platelets are sticky?"

"I might have a Protein S deficiency."

"How do you—"

"I researched it. I tracked the symptoms back to the source. It's a cause of a pulmonary embolism, when a blood clot in the leg breaks off and travels to the lung."

"A doctor told you you had this?"

"Doctor Google told me. I had a pain right here, in the middle of my thigh. Then all of a sudden it was gone. It was so small it had to be a clot. I had most of the symptoms; rapid breathing, chest pains when I inhaled, palpitations. I'm still waiting for sudden death. I hope I get a few minutes warning, to lie down first so I don't fall and hit my head."

"Are you sick often?"

"Not sick, exactly. I have symptoms every day. Sometimes twice a day. I don't think my hypochondria has been correctly diagnosed."

"You think it's hypochondria?"

"Maybe."

"When did it start?'

"A couple years ago."

Phil scratched inside his ear, thinking.

"That could be a fungal infection," Jason said. "If you mix equal parts of white vinegar and rubbing alcohol, you can squeeze it from a cotton ball into your ear. But just do it a couple times a day or your ear will dry out and your canal will be flakey."

"That's good to know."

"Yeah, well, we have to know these days."

"You don't like doctors, I take it."

"I don't like how they work. They don't put the symptoms together. They stay in their own little specialized cubbyholes and if they can't find what's wrong they pass you along to the next cubbyhole. We're not whole people anymore, we're Pep Boys body parts, ball joints to air bags. Tell them what leaks, what smells, if we're sluggish, misfiring, whatever ails us, when did it start, when's the last time we had service. They hoist us up on a lift and check the place they specialize in and if that part's okay, down we come, off to the next cubicle. When I was growing up we had a family doctor, Doctor Yuengling. He handled everything; nosebleeds, rashes, sprains, surgery, whatever. He knew it when I had appendicitis. He connected the dots. I don't suppose you have any beer. That Reuben made me thirsty."

"How about an iced cappuccino?"

"Why do they call it iced? There's no such thing as *iced cappuccino*. Cappuccino is one third expresso, one third steamed milk and one third foam. If you put ice in it, it would be disgusting and pointless."

"Do you want one?"

119

"Sure."

"That's interesting," Phil said, "that you seem to know when your health situation changed."

"That doesn't have anything to do with the way things are now. Got something wrong? Extreme pain in your whatever and you call your doctor? *'We can't see you for three weeks. If it's an emergency, go to the ER like everybody else.'* So, you go and sit for three hours huddled in your chair surrounded by all this hacking and bleeding and rocking and crying and groaning and scratching and puking and shaking and detoxing and arguing—

'I told you not to climb that fucking ladder!'—'It's your fault the condom came off. Now I'm the one who has to go in there so they can find it!'—'It was bad crack, man. They sold me bad crack.'—'I'll never hit you again. I promise.'—'I don't know how it got stuck in there!' —

"And just when you think it's your turn, somebody on a stretcher is rushed in ahead of you. Bleeding people are always treated better. So, you hug your gut and know that you have, in fact, died and gone straight to hell, until your name is called and you finally make it back to a room with nice clean curtains, knowing all your pain and suffering will disappear when they insert the magic needle. So you tell them where you hurt, a ten on a pain scale of one to ten, and the doctor comes in, looks in your mouth, says you have gingivitis, gives you a pill and a scrip and tells you to go see your family doctor.

"So you get an appointment three weeks away and pop Tylenol when the prescription is gone until you go in and the nurse weighs you and takes your blood pressure and tells you the doctor will be right in and shuts the door, and you sit on the end of the examination table with your feet dangling like a kid in a highchair, checking out the jars of cotton balls and tongue depressors and the big glossy laminated color poster of your digestive system and the layers of your large intestine and how your liver looks like a purple Nazi helmet.

"And you look for dust balls or blood splatters the cleaning people might have missed, while your nose starts to freeze and drip while you listen to other doors opening and closing out in the hall, but not yours, not yet, but maybe the next time. And finally a half hour later you hear somebody pick up your file from the slot outside the door and the door finally opens and no matter how pissed you are, you smile and hold out your shriveled cold fingers to shake hands.

"And they ask how you're doing but they're not looking at you, they're typing and looking at a computer screen and asking you questions and you point to where it hurts and they glance for two seconds, then go back to the *computer* you, not the *you* you. Then finally after typing for five minutes they listen to your heart and tap on your back and look in your ears and feel your glands and tell you on the way out the door that they're referring you to an ENT specialist and the nurse will set it up.

"So you pop more Tylenol and wait for that appointment and if they don't find anything, they send you to a rhinologist, who sends you to a neurologist, who sends you to an ophthalmologist, who sends you to an allergist, who sends you to a dentist who at least cleans your teeth. Every one of them, even if they're in the same field, will prescribe something different. And every one of them wants to run expensive tests.

"It takes two months to get an appointment with each of these specialists—who become specialists because they make twice as much money as primary care doctors, by the way—which is why there aren't enough regular doctors anymore—but it takes two months to get in, after the schedulers grill you about your insurance, which they may or may not accept. At the end of a year you've seen six specialists, or subspecialists, and you're either dead, have enough drugs to start your own cartel or you Googled a forum where you can at least share war stories. You know what the consensus is? Why people feel depressed and shafted? Because if the doctors can't find it, it's because A: there's nothing wrong with you; B: it's psychosomatic and you need to see a psychiatrist, or C: you're fat and need to lose weight."

"You've never been fat, have you?"

"That's what people on the forums have been told, A, B or C. Doctors should go in there and read some of it. Maybe something would change. But it won't. They insulate themselves in their little tubes, like cocoons. Got pain? Deal with it. Doctors won't admit they just don't know. That's why people are Googling their symptoms now. Google *itching* and see how many diseases you might have.

"I know I've gone overboard on the self-diagnosing, but when you don't get answers, when you're blown off from one doctor to the next, you have to feel like you're doing something to help yourself. Ignored pain is your body's way of telling you your doctor is an asshole."

"When you—"

"Healthcare is like entering the Twilight Zone. We're travelling in another dimension, the middle ground between science and guessing. I had a pain, okay, in the lower right side of my abdomen, way down here, close to where my appendix was. I never had this doctor before; he's one in a group that rotates, a real frost bag. Wouldn't look me in the eye, shuffled around, half-assed backward exam. I tried to explain what was going on and he finally says, *'I can get to the problem a lot sooner if you'll be quiet.'* It was so ridiculous I actually laughed. His face got red but at least he ordered an ultrasound, which I wanted.

"So I went in and they prepped me way up here, on my right side, practically under my rib cage. I said, '*I don't have any problems up here. I hurt down here.*' And I showed them, so they looked at the doctor's order and they said the order was for a liver scan and they could only do the test the doctor ordered.

"A few days later I got a call from the doctor's office and they said, '*Good news, your liver looks fine.*' I said, '*Yeah but, that's not why I went in there.*' And they said, '*Well, we don't know anything about that. Would you like to make an appointment?*' I said, '*Yes. I'd like an appointment with Dr. Yuengling. He's dead now, but I'll wait.*'"

He leaned back and threw up his hands. "That's what's out there. And just wait till Trumpcare kicks in. It's already leaked that the premiums won't cover an ass boil unless you have the Golden Trumpcare plan. He's doling it out to the highest pay-to-players and loving every minute of it, watching them kill each other to get in the game, like Nero watching the gladiators. Nero burned two-thirds of Rome because he wanted to build elaborate palaces and villas and call it Neropolis. Remind you of anybody?"

Phil nodded, rubbing his hands together. He looked uncomfortable.

"What's the matter? Is one of your family a doctor?"

"No." He sighed heavily. "I need to make a confession to you."

"Okay."

"What's the term for craving a cigarette so bad right now, I could chew the barrel off my gun."

Jason smirked. "Nic fit. You can smoke if you want."

"No. I quit. One month and five days ago. Right now I could smoke a foot-long cigarette in one drag. One long, hot, glowing, tobacco-sizzling ash. I'd suck that cancer stick clear down to my toenails."

"Sounds rough."

"I've been hitting Snickers pretty hard this month. I may be testing out your fat patient theory if I don't knock off the snacking."

"Not a theory. What does it feel like, detoxing?"

"For the first few days, it feels like being two seconds away from an orgasm. You're right on the brink and you know that with just one more right move, every pleasurable nerve in your body will explode. The dam will burst. And you wait for it. And wait for it. But it doesn't happen. You can't pull the trigger. The gun is locked. You break into a cold sweat. It's actual pain, except it's not in your groin, it's inside your chest. Your veins start to ache and you want to hit something. Hard! Then you say something rotten and stupid to your wife and she tells you to go fuck yourself—which you would do if it would help, but it wouldn't, you'd just want a cigarette even more. And after about fifteen minutes the intensity eases off, until the next time. In between you feel various degrees of frustrated."

"How often does that happen?"

"The worst ones are almost constant the first couple days. Then it starts tapering down to a couple times a day, then once a day. Right now it's about every three or four days, but they don't last as long."

"Want to hear a joke?"

"Sure. Anything, till this passes."

"A chicken and an egg are lying in bed. The chicken is leaning back against the headboard, smoking a cigarette with a satisfied smile on its face. The egg gives it a dirty look, rolls over and says, *'Well! I guess we finally answered that question.'*"

Phil thought a moment, then burst out laughing. "So, the chicken came first. Good one."

"Is it getting any better?"

"No. Sometimes I have to walk it off."

Jason thought a moment. "How about we make a deal?"

Phil waited.

"You go outside," Jason said, "walk it off, and I'll check my phone for messages."

"Sorry."

"Just let me have it for one minute. I want to make a quick call to Amy and make sure she got home okay."

"No."

"That's kind of like being an asshole, Phil. I'm only asking for thirty seconds. It's my dime."

"It's my dime now. So, no."

Jason angrily slapped the desk, then grabbed his wrist. "Ow! Damn! I think I broke it." He cradled the injury in his hand and rocked it back and forth. "Not that you care."

"You're right. I don't. I appreciate this fresh insight into your personality, however. You must get away with a lot."

"Not recently. Do you have an arm sling in one of those drawers? You've got everything else in there."

"Do you want an aspirin?"

"Do you want my answer?"

"Do you want to act like a baby or get back to business?"

Jason massaged his wrist and said nothing.

"Let's go back to where we left off. Anything more you want to say about Trumpcare?"

"It won't matter. We're all going to die horrible deaths anyway. Trump cut funding to the CDC that fights global disease outbreaks in other countries; Ebola, malaria, cholera, the plague. He slashed it by eighty percent before he crowned himself, but back then he just wanted to keep the money for his pet ass-kissers. Now it's one of his ways to keep his peasants from leaving. If we fly overseas we'll catch some epidemic and bring it back here, infect the worker colony. That would hurt his Comprehensive Deathcare Plan. If we die we can't pay his monthly burial premium. He just wants us braindead."

"That reminds me," Phil said. He removed a stack of cards from his desk. "This is kind of a fun personality test. I'll show you an image and you tell me what you see."

"The Rorschach test?"

"Yes. Give me your first impression, don't think about it." Phil held up the first card. "What do you see when you look at this image?"

"Hips. Evil hips. A teeny weeny."

"Okay. What about this one?"

"A goofy guy with a big mouth. Laughing. Or maybe he's having oral sex. Yeah, that one. Pretty graphic, actually."

"Okay. What do you see here?"

"Two dudes dancing around a cauldron. Probably Trump and Putin. Two hearts so they're in love. Music notes on each side so they're singing to each other or playing romantic music."

"This?"

"A monster with a big tail with pincers on the end, jumping down on me. Can't get away. It's too close. Big feet going to knock me down first." He thought a moment. "I guess that's all."

"All right. What about this?"

"A bat, carrying a sword and an assault rifle in each wing."

"This?"

"A flattened bobcat with big whiskers, like it's been run over by a tank, spread out on a floor or a wall, like a trophy. Probably next to elephant tails and body parts of other unarmed wild animals killed for sport by rich heartless assholes. Go to the next card. This one is really pissing me off."

"Okay. Here."

"Two women who want to kiss each other. They both look identical. Actually, it looks like Ivanka. She's getting ready to kiss herself in a mirror."

Phil revealed the next card.

"Two big pink rats, one on each side, climbing up the shoulders of something that's rising out of something orange and pink, could be flames. The two rats are holding the thing's hands and are climbing up to get on its shoulders, so they can both be on top, Kings of everything. You want to know what's going to happen next?"

"No. Just tell me what you see. What about this?"

Jason blew out his breath. "It's two demons made out of flames, laughing and celebrating about something, kind of dancing around in some weird smoke."

"Last one."

"Two blue crabs fighting. There are two small angry creatures between them, in hand combat. Two red seahorses are holding hands, watching the battle. Things are scattered, maybe broken off. Like everything's hitting the fan." He stared a few moments longer. "That's it."

"Okay! That was good." Phil stacked the cards and returned them to the drawer.

"So? What's the diagnosis?"

"You're pissed."

They both laughed.

"That's the story of my life in ten flashcards," Jason said. He stared tiredly at the window. "I feel like there's a giant web over the whole country and there's this small group of rich, greedy spiders high up in this control room and they jiggle the threads where it will bring in the most money."

He plucked the air with his fingertips. "Twing—*Massive Lies?* Twang—*Alternative Facts.* Twing—*Bribery?* Twang— *Loyalty.* Twing—*Global warming?* Twang—*The Mexicans brought it across the border.*"

He smirked. "I paid two thousand dollars to bitch about this shit, and I am going to bitch."

Phil nodded. "Glad I don't have to pry it out of you."

"Nope," Jason replied. "Press any button."

—8—

"How does Amy feel about your health issues?"

"She thinks I'm a hypochondriac. She takes my temperature with an éclair."

"She sounds fun."

"Yeah. Good cook, too, like her mother. They're going to kill me. They're not into health issues. Or rather, *my* health issues."

"Because they're not an issue, Jason. You're not sick." Amy removed a container from the fridge and scooped a spoonful of white lard into a heated frying pan. It immediately dissolved into clear liquid and flowed across the bottom.

An orange tabby leaped up onto a bar stool and sat intently, watching her cook. "Mommy will feed you a nice yummy treat in just a few minutes, baby," she cooed. Kit-Kat meowed and purred.

"I didn't say I was sick," Jason said. "I said I thought I might be sick. I just thought my eyes looked unusually red. You didn't look. You glanced."

Amy leaned in close, narrowing her eyes, peering hard from one eye to the other. "They're fine. You're fine. Stop looking in the mirror."

He rubbed his left shoulder and watched her layer thinly sliced potatoes and onions into the hot grease. They immediately began to sizzle and emit delicious, gut-rumbling aromas. "That smells wonderful," he said, hoping to temper the next remark. "I just wish lard wasn't so bad for our health."

"It isn't."

"It's lard."

"Is the food greasy when you eat it?"

"No."

"Can you taste it?"

"No. But the taste isn't the problem. It's the fat. It's making me fat."

"Gee, you don't think it's from the bags of chips and beer and cookies and beer and peanut-butter cups and pizza and beer you eat."

"Lard clogs your arteries."

"No. It does not. Trans-fats clog your arteries. I'm ready for you this time, Jason. You're not the only one who knows how to Google." She ground salt and pepper over the crisping food in angry twists of her wrist. "Nana is eighty-seven and she's in perfect health. She's been cooking with lard all her life. My mother and father were raised on it and they're both fine. People all over the world use it and

they're a lot healthier than we are. I don't buy the stuff from the grocery store. That's hydrogenated. This is leaf lard. It's good stuff, Jason. Leave it alone. Leave me alone. Go away and let me make dinner in peace." Kit-Kat jumped off the stool and darted from the room.

"Yeah but, shortening is vegetable oil."

"Vegetables don't have oil." She reached for a glass of red wine and took a swallow. "I can't believe we're having this argument again. I know you were raised on the canned factory stuff. If you enjoy eating hydrogenated globs of palm oil, then by all means, eat it. I hesitate to point out the obvious to you, Jason, but your father dropped dead from a heart attack when he was sixty-two." She shrugged. "Just sayin'."

"That was a mean blow," he uttered. He rubbed his left arm.

"Oh for god's sake, will you stop that? You are not having a heart attack. Your eyes are not red. You do not have a fever. I am going to take that book away from you!"

"What book is that?" Phil interrupted.

"Preston's *The Hot Zone.* It's the most horrifying nonfiction book I've ever read. It's about filoviruses, Ebola and other viruses, like swarms of invisible monsters mutating and getting stronger, ready to ravage and kill us in horrible ways in a few days and free the planet of human parasites."

Phil cringed. "Okay. Go ahead."

"It's not the book's fault we're facing a very real threat to life as we know it, not counting Trump," he told her.

"Is it supposed to ruin our lives now? Before it happens? If it happens?"

"Not if. It's out there, waiting for meat."

"Thank you for ruining dinner. This is all we're having now. Potatoes and onions."

"And animal fat."

"Goddammit, Jason. Then throw it out! I'm taking a bath and going to bed." She flipped off the burner, snatched the glass of wine from the counter and stalked out.

"Where's your sense of humor?" he called after her. "I was kidding!" He waited. "I'm feeling better now. Seriously!" Loud music from the bedroom radio drowned him out. He gingerly peeled off a hot, crispy slice of potato, then another, then got a fork and ate directly from the frying pan.

The phone rang. It was picked up after one ring, before he could check the caller ID. The receiver indicated the phone was in use. She was probably in there crying to her mother, telling her what a shit he was. She was right.

Jason got a plate from the cupboard and put a scoop of fried potatoes in the center. With the edge of a spoon he carefully sculpted a perfect shape of a heart. He put a large fresh tomato on the cutting board, sliced and cubed it, and arranged the bright red bits in a neat outline around the heart-shaped sculpture. He studied and tweaked his masterpiece, then went to the fridge, found a green onion stalk in the vegetable bin and lanced it through the center of the heart. Beautiful. Candle? No. Overkill. He grabbed the wine bottle, a glass and the potato peace-offering and found her sitting on the edge of the bed, still talking on the phone.

"I have to go now," she muttered into the receiver. "Thanks for calling." She hung up and glared at him, stoic, frozen, wronged.

Jason sat down on the bed, a foot away from her, and offered forth the plate. Her mouth jerked once, staring at it. "I love you," he said meekly. "I'm sorry. I love your potatoes. These are all that are left. I made an absolute pig of myself eating them. I am filled with delicious food and remorse. Can you ever forgive me?"

For a brief second he thought he detected a grin. "That is the silliest thing I've ever seen," she said.

"But it's heartfelt." Her shoulders and jawline began to thaw. He set the plate gently on her lap, in front of her clinched fists. "I'm thoughtless and *completely undeserving of your forgiveness. I am totally at fault. One-hundred percent. All the way, entirely, whole hog—no reference to the lard."*

She held up her hand to stop him, smiled tiredly, then closed her eyes and shook her head. "I don't know what to do with you, Jason. I'm not equipped for you."

"Oh god. Yes, you are. Your equipment is amazing."

"Emotionally, I mean." She thawed completely, her eyes filling with tears. "You are so infuriating! You're paranoid about everything! I don't know how to argue with you. I don't understand half the stuff you're talking about."

"I don't either. I was hoping you could tell me."

She laughed, wiping tears away with the back of her hand. Kit-Kat appeared at her feet, staring up at the cooling plate of food. "I'm not hungry," she said to Jason. "Can she have it?"

"Sure. Sorry I forgot a fork."

"No you didn't." She set the plate on the floor. A second later they were kissing violently, pulling off clothes, clutching and groping and moaning as the bra unhooked and shoes hit the floor.

Kit-Kat licked the plate clean, curled up on her pillow, watched the wild antics on the bed with a bored expression for a few seconds, then drifted off to sleep.

The room was getting dark when the fever finally broke into a cool, contented sweat. Jason bundled her in his arms in a protective spoon and kissed behind her ear.

"I guess you should call your mother back," he said.

"My mother?"

"Tell her I came to my senses."

"What do you mean?"

"Weren't you talking to her on the phone when I came in?"

"Oh." She paused, thinking. "No." *Her voice was fake casual.*

"Oh. Okay. I just thought." *He had the sense God gave a goat and kept his mouth shut. He kissed her shoulder, snuggled closer and smiled with a sigh of contentment.*

Amy waited for the next question. It didn't happen. His arms were relaxing, his breathing slow and measured. What the hell was going on? He was going to sleep? She readjusted, pulling up a cover, enough to drag him back from a fast-moving doze.

"No," she said, "it wasn't mother. The call wasn't anything. I don't want you to feel upset or anything."

"Was it the IRS? Then I don't give a shit."

"It was an old friend of mine. Mel Stiner."

"That's nice. Everything all right with her?"

"She's a he. Melvin. Melvin Stiner."

He mulled this over a second. One crises was just averted. Stay the hell out of another one, Jason. Hug her and go to sleep.

"How did he get my number?" he asked anyway.

"Mother gave it to him. She knows we're just friends now."

"How long have you been friends?"

"A couple years."

"A couple years counting the time you were lovers, or after you were lovers and then you became friends?"

"I never said we were lovers. I said we were old friends. Why would you assume we were lovers?"

"I don't know, Amy. I was drifting off to sleep and had an image of your hand on his thigh."

She froze. "I can't believe you just said that." She clambered out of bed and yanked a sheet around her. The glare was back, fiery, indignant. "I cannot believe you just said that!"

"What did I say?" He got out of bed and raised his hands to the heavens. "What did I say wrong? We've both had sex with other people before we met. I have never been jealous of your past boyfriends. Well maybe a little bit, but that's just human. You've asked about my old girlfriends. You were a little jealous. I could tell. That's normal. I was just saying."

"Will you please put some clothes on? I cannot have a decent argument with you with your empty penis hanging there like that."

He found his briefs under the blanket and pulled them on. "Just for the record," he said, "you started this one. I didn't ask you who called. When you said it wasn't your mother, I let it drop. You made a point—a point!— of letting me know it was an old boyfriend. Whatever's going on now is something you wanted. You wanted some reaction from me. Just cut to the god-damn chase and tell me, Amy. What is this all about?"

Her chin lifted, her eyes narrowed. "I wanted to know if you were thinking about me or the latest horrible thing Trump has done now."

"Things. Plural."

"Yes! Thank you! I know we've had this argument before, but it just bugs me, Jason. I can't help it! When we're done making love, are you still holding me or off somewhere stressing over your massive stockpile of doom and gloom—Trump's cover-ups, treason, global epidemics, Russian hacking, dictators, money laundering, porn-star payoffs, banana republics, mob rule, mass destruction. What's the point of any of this then, Jason, of you and me, if we have no future? Are we going anywhere? What do you want? Where am I in the middle of all this? Is there ever a minute when

you're not obsessing about what maybe, possibly, remotely might happen?"

He stared at her a full minute, thinking. She glared, waiting. He cleared his throat. "I know I'm concerned about other things, but I don't obsess. I'm vigilant. I'm taking necessary precautions . . ."

"You don't obsess?" She stalked over to the closet as best she could, clutching the sheet about her with one hand. She flung open the door. "You don't obsess?" She pulled out a tall cardboard box. "Then explain some of this to me." She lifted out a cellophane-wrapped package and held it up. "What's this?"

"It's a full face NBC respirator to protect us from nuclear, biological, chemical agents—nerve gas, anthrax, SARS, plague, cholera. There's one in there for you, too. Trump's trying to cut billions from health programs, the FDA. Hello, trichinosis."

"What's this thing?"

"Polyethylene coveralls, for chemical and nuclear fallout. Okay, those are PVC boots. Those are nitrile gloves. Plastic sheeting. You can see that's duct tape. A tube tent. That's a hazmat suit— hazardous materials suit. Extra socks. HELP flag."

"What's in this other big box?"

"Triage kits, trauma bags, a hammock, blizzard bag, solar light bulb, GI mess kit, crowbar, medical kit, foot powder, bug repellant, bear spray, sinus flush."

She stared at him. "You're serious."

"We have to have this stuff if we hope to survive, Amy. Everybody's buying it. That's what I've been trying to tell you."

"Wow. Okay. What else is in there?"

"Fire-starter paste, a wire saw, mayday mirror, survivor seeds, radio-flashlight, body warmers, slingshot, compass, can opener, ponchos, water filter, Garden-In-A-Can, dental floss, dehydrated water, axe, whistle, boat horn, snow shoes, home canning supplies. We could use a solar oven. I can't remember what else."

"Dehydrated water?"

"I was seeing if you were paying attention."

"And the stuff under the bed is all food?"

"Mostly soup. A few cans of ravioli." He watched her shove the box back into the closet. "A lot of those things I have two of, for both of us. Us, Amy. I'm expecting another order to come in next week. It has a solar-heated shower, just for you. If war breaks out, I'll get Amazon Prime. Guaranteed two-day delivery. They're working to get delivery drones. Thirty minutes and it's on our doorstep. If North Korea launches, I could place a last-minute order and we'd have it and be out of here before it hits."

She smiled faintly and shook her head.

"And I'll buy lard," he said. "A tub of leaf lard so we can fry roots and bugs in our own little cave somewhere. We can hunt and forage under rocks and rotten logs. Yum! Fried grubs! M-m-m-m. Sautéed grasshoppers. We should leave now and beat the apocalypse rush."

She smirked. "Shut up."

He ambled over to her side of the bed and sat down. "I obsess about us, Amy. I swear to God, I wouldn't give a shit about anything if I didn't have you."

"This is all pretty incredible, Jason. I don't know what to think. You must not be crazy if they're selling this stuff."

"By the truckload! Freeze-dried linguine is on backorder."

She shrugged. "Okay."

"Okay. Good." He paused a long moment, until the fallout finished settling. "So, what's the deal with this guy Melvin? Kinda ballsy, calling my woman at my house."

"She grinned, threw the sheet at him and headed for the bathroom. "I have to pee."

"Did you tell him my hands are lethal weapons? I have a belt. I have moves I've never shown anyone. They're so dangerous I had to register my hands and feet. They have tracking devices. You want to see jealous, Amy? I'll show you jealous."

When she came out of the bathroom, he was holding a bucket of Ghirardelli chocolate. "I made dinner," he said.

"Snowshoes?" Phil asked.

"Oh yeah. I have maps of previous ice age glacier patterns. We can only hope we live south of the permafrost line. Scientists are saying the polar ice cap is going to melt. God knows how bad that will be. It depends on where it happens."

"So, you actually have all this gear?"

"For basic catastrophes and cataclysms. If there's a shift in the earth's axis or a reversal of geo-magnetic fields or a large meteor strike, we're fucked."

—9—

You said your father died suddenly from a heart attack."

"Yes. He did."

"Were you there when it happened?"

"No. I was home. My mother called me."

"Do you remember what you thought when she told you?"

"I didn't think anything then. She just called and asked if I could come over."

"She didn't say why?"

"No. I figured it was one of her hug calls. If her social life wasn't going right she always needed a hug from her baby. I'm her baby. *'At least my baby loves me.'* Cry-cry sniff-sniff. That sort of thing."

"No brothers or sisters?"

"Nope. Just me. When I was born my father slapped the doctor. No more kids. Just our cozy little threesome." He shifted in the chair, trying to find a comfortable position, crossing his legs, uncrossing them. He shot an irritated glance at Phil. "Can we move on, now?"

"No. So, you went over to your parents' house. Right away? Right after your mother called you?"

"A few minutes after."

"What time did she call?"

"It was about two in the afternoon."

"How far away was their house?"

"Sammamish."

Phil nodded. Lakes, parks, suburban elite. "So, you went over there, and . . . how did you find out? What did she tell you?"

"I rang the doorbell and she answered the door and I said, 'Where's the party?'"

"Why—"

"She was dressed up, like she was going out to dinner or to the club. She was holding a tissue to her nose, but it didn't look like she'd been crying. She was very nervous. I asked her what the matter was."

"Oh, Jason! Something ghastly has happened!"

Beverly Nickle grabbed her son in a quick hug, then dabbed the crumpled tissue beneath a dry eye. A hint of Joy perfume touched his nose, a scent, she often enjoyed explaining, requiring the sacrifice of three-hundred and thirty-six roses and ten-thousand jasmine flowers *to produce one golden ounce. She was thin, stylish, with perfectly coifed and molded salt-and-pepper hair. The mauve rouge and heavy eyeliner made her look much older than her sixty-one years.*

145

"What's going on?" Jason asked.

"Oh, Jason. I don't know how to tell you. Your father is dead! He died! He's dead." She nodded toward a distant room. "In there."

"Geezus. Mother. I'm sorry!"

"Do you want to see him?"

"No. Yes. I guess." He followed her reluctantly across the polished hardwood floors, over the antique Persian rug, into the handsomely decorated family room, a term he had always found amusing since 'the family' had never sat in it at the same time. The TV was turned off, the tall draperies half drawn, the air eerily quiet and strange. His father, wearing dark blue silk pajamas, sat slumped in his favorite black leather armchair, mouth drooped open, eyes closed, his right hand still gripping the remote. Jason stared at him a full minute without speaking. "He's purple," he said at last.

"Yes. It's been getting worse. His hair is starting to stick out. It's been just ghastly, Jason. I don't know what to do."

"What happened? Did you find him like this?"

"Yes. I was in the kitchen making coffee. He was watching the news. They were showing clips of something about Obama or something with the democrats and he was yelling and getting upset. I told him to turn the channel, but it was Fox News. If we watch any other news we're not Christian or decent Americans. We must only listen to them,

146

Jason! I heard him shout, 'Card carrying commie!'
and then it got very quiet. I had my juice and a half
cup of raison bran and it was still quiet. I called and
asked him if he wanted coffee and he didn't answer.
I thought maybe he didn't hear me, so I came in here
and found him . . . like that. The television was off.
He must have turned it off, the last thing he did
before . . . dying." She pressed the tissue to her
mouth, looking genuinely frightened. "Oh Jason, I
don't know what to do. I have been in an absolute
state all day."

"All day? When did it happen?"

"This morning."

"This morning! What time this morning?"

"I don't know the exact minute. I hadn't had
coffee yet. It must have been about eight o'clock."

He glanced at his watch. "It's a quarter to
three. You didn't call nine-one-one?"

"Well, no Jerome. I couldn't call them yet. I
was still in my pajamas. I needed to take a shower
and get dressed. And call you. Good heavens, I
couldn't have strangers coming into the house that
early. The neighbors would come over to see what
was going on. I had to be ready."

"How did you know for sure he was dead?
Maybe he just had a stroke or passed out or
something."

She shook her head. "A wife knows. When you get married, your wife will know when you're dead."

"Did you feel for a pulse?"

"Not exactly. I poked his arm with my finger several times and said his name. He was starting to get cold. He was so skinny, you know. He didn't have anything to hold the body heat in."

Jason sat down on the floor facing the chair holding his father's remains. He stared at him, rubbed his forehead, took several deep breaths, stared again. "Geezus," he said more than once.

"I didn't know what to do," Beverly repeated in a pleading tone. Jason just didn't seem to understand the difficult position she was in, the unwritten social protocol in situations like this. She would be the center of attention, stared at, pitied, whispered about. Her shoes would be judged, her clothes, her demeanor. He had no right to act as though she had done something wrong.

"What were you feeling right then, Jason? Phil interrupted. "When you were sitting on the floor, staring at him."

"Shock, I guess. It was hard to believe he was really dead. I remember thinking, this is it, it's over. He's never going to like me and I'm never going to like him. What a fucking waste."

"Of what?"

148

"Family. Home. I was the kitchen, he was the bathroom. We never had a living room. My mother was the façade, the window dressing."

"That's a little . . .harsh, isn't it? It sounds like she really was confused at the time. In shock, like you."

"Maybe. There's more."

"It doesn't matter when I call the authorities, does it, Jason?" Beverly asked. "I mean, it's not like this is a murder scene. He just died in his own home. We have a right to spend time with him alone, to say our goodbyes. Some people dress the bodies and everything, get them ready for company."

"This isn't the prairie, mother. We're not Amish. If you couldn't even take his pulse, how are you going to change his clothes?"

"Well no. I couldn't." She stared expectantly at him.

He tried to wrap his brain around it. "You're not seriously suggesting that you want me to prepare him for the authorities!"

"Not completely. If you could just shave him first, before anyone sees him like this. Maybe slip on a nice suit . . ."

His jaw dropped open. "Are you out of your fucking mind?" He held up his hand to silence her, climbing to his feet. "Listen to me, mother. Number one, it is illegal to move his body before the

149

authorities see him. Number two, what you did—
what you didn't do!—was negligent, maybe
criminally negligent. Regular people, family
members, are not qualified to determine if
somebody is really dead. A doctor has to determine
that, or a medical examiner. He was probably dead
when you found him, he was probably dead,
mother, but you didn't know that for a fact. You
found him slumped here like this, you did not take
his pulse, you went upstairs, took a shower,
changed your clothes . . .why did you put on a
cocktail dress?"

"It's my best black. I put on slacks and a new
blouse, but it didn't seem respectful, so I changed
into this. Are the pearls too much?"

"What else did you do? You didn't call me until
two and you found him about eight-thirty. It didn't
take you five and a half hours to shower and change
your clothes. What else did you do?" She twisted the
tissue and didn't answer. "Mother?"

"I . . . well, I went to the bank. I heard that
bank accounts can be closed until a death is settled
so I withdrew some money."

"How much?"

"You know I don't discuss our personal
finances."

"Part of the balance? Half?"

Her lips trembled. She stared at him.

"You drained the account, mother?"

"No. I didn't. I left twenty-five dollars."

"Where did you go after that?"

She lifted her chin defiantly. "Shopping."

"You shopped? Dad's lying here dead and you went to Nordstrom?"

"No, I did not go to Nordstrom. And I resent your tone. I needed more Ativan. I was hyperventilating, and I only had two pills left so I went to Walgreens and had to wait while it was refilled, and I needed black pantyhose. I came straight home and took a pill and waited for the bubbles around my heart to calm down, then I called you."

He closed his eyes. "Oh geezus, this is going to look like murder."

"Well it is not, Jason! When they do the autopsy, they'll see it was his heart."

"But you were required to report it to the police and paramedics. He might have been alive. Maybe only a little, but enough."

"But I have an Advanced Directive. He didn't want to be kept alive by artificial means."

"That's if there's no hope, mother. That's after the doctors have done all they can for him and anything else would be artificial. It's the paramedic's job to try to revive him and get him to the hospital so the doctors can decide that he's dead. Except if he's obviously been dead a long time, like now, and rigor mortis is setting in, which it is, which only happens hours after he's dead. That's why his hair and beard are starting to stick out."

Her hands flew to her mouth. "I can't breathe!" she shrieked. "I can't breathe! My heart is racing! Help me, Jason. I'm smothering! I'm going to faint!"

Jason quickly helped her to a nearby sofa. "Where's your Ativan? In your purse? Where is it? Upstairs? On your dresser? Keep breathing into your hands. I'll be right back." He tore up the winding stairway two steps at a time and returned with the vial and glass of water in less than a minute. Her hands were shaking violently. He put the small white pill in her mouth and she gulped down the water. "Okay, now just lean over, mother, and breathe into your hands. Take a breath, count to five. Let it out. That's good. Take a breath, count to five. Let it out. That's good. Just breathe slowly and relax. I'm right here."

She was shivering so badly he put a sofa throw around her shoulders and patted her arm, his mind racing. They would have to lie. If the authorities heard the real story they might call it negligent homicide. They might call this a crime scene now. They'd find the prescription bottle, freshly filled. They'd find the cash in her purse—he'd seen the envelope when he retrieved the pills; an obscene wad of thousand dollar bills. They'd check the bank and think she was planning to run. She'd look guilty as sin. She'd swallow the whole bottle if she knew the trouble she was in. Okay, so, what could the lie be? The simpler the better. Occam's razor: all things being equal, the simplest explanation tends to be the right one.

Fifteen minutes later he asked, "Are you feeling better now, mother?"

She straightened up and nodded feebly. "Thank you, Jason. I don't know what I'd do without my baby." She patted his hand.

He felt very sorry for her. She tried her best. She really did. "I've been thinking about this, mother, and this is what we need to say. What you need to say, when the paramedics get here. It's very simple. Are you ready to hear this now or do you want to wait a few more minutes?"

"No, I want to hear it now. Go ahead."

"You need to tell them that you came down for breakfast, as usual, and you heard him in here watching television. He'd said he was going to play golf later this morning—"

"I can't say that. His friends would have called when he didn't show up. The phone would show no one called."

Sometimes she impressed the hell out of him. "You're right, mother. Yes. Okay, say he said he wanted to polish his gun collection this morning in his den, and you needed to do your own shopping, so after breakfast you got dressed and came

153

downstairs and called to him that you were going shopping. The television was still on and you went on out. When you got back you could hear the television was off so you thought he was in his den. You didn't come into this room until about two-thirty and you found him, like that."

They glanced at the body. It looked even more dead. They quickly looked away, feeling pangs of guilt.

"And you found him," Jason continued, "and you immediately called me, and I came over and took his pulse and it was obvious he'd been dead a while, and we immediately called nine-one-one. Okay? Now repeat that to me, the way you'll say it to them."

"Should I tell them about the bank?"

"No. They won't check anything like that. If they do, if the subject comes up, say you were afraid of a stock market crash and you wanted to have more money available at home. A lot of people are doing that now. Okay, tell me what you're going to say."

Beverly did a flawless run-through, then looked at him with pleading eyes. "He really was dead, Jason. I know with all my heart, he was dead."

"I'm sure you're right, mother." He stood and rubbed his hands together. They were cold. His heart hammered against his chest. His breathing

was labored. "I'm going to call now. I doubt they'll bother with the hospital. They'll probably take him to the Medical Examiner's office to determine the cause of death. Do you want to practice again?"

"No. I just want to get this over with!"

"Okay, here we go." He tapped nine-one-one into the family room phone.

"No problems, I take it," Phil said.

"No. They came out pretty fast, the police and fire department. Somebody else came out, I think it was the coroner, I don't know, but they finally zipped him up and took him away. Mother and I didn't stay in the room. As soon as the cops got there, we went and sat in the kitchen. We drank water. She said he, my father, was lucky—she told me, not the cops! She said he lived a lot longer than she thought he would. It was all very unreal.

"Mother was right about the neighbors coming over. I told them she couldn't see anyone yet. They were trying to peek past me, over my shoulder, to see what was going on. The whole thing was very . . .I don't know. Grotesque, in a way. We weren't even crying. Neither one of us. They probably thought we were in shock, the police I mean. We were, I guess. I have no idea what my mother was thinking, about him being dead. They'd been married for thirty-five years." He shrugged. "Anyway, she passed Go but didn't go to

155

jail. She moved to Florida." He held out his hands. "And here I am. The rest is a mystery."

"Question."

"Okay."

"Do you know what your mother meant when she said your father was lucky? That's a rather unusual comment to make about someone who died suddenly."

"I didn't know what she meant when she said it, no." Jason glanced at the floor, the window, the entry door, the oil painting of ships.

"Did you think it was strange?"

He nodded. "Yeah."

"But you didn't ask anything about it?"

"Yeah. Later I did. After everybody was gone I had a couple shots of Maker's Mark whiskey. Good stuff. Handmade. Every batch is taste-tested more than five times before it's bottled. I should get a job there. Fuck Peeper's Sleepers."

"What did she say?"

"Who?"

"Your mother, when you asked her what she meant."

"It was later that night. She was in her cups. We were sitting in the living room, in front of a fire. She said, *'Well, Jason, at least he lived twenty-five years longer than anyone ever expected.'* I said, *'What do you mean? He was never sick.'* She said, *'Because all the Nickle men die young.'* I said, *'How* young?' And she said, *'In their thirties. His father, his grandfather, his great grandfather, all the men on the paternal side died of heart attacks in their thirties.'* She looked at me and started to cry. *'We've worked so hard to keep it from you. But you have a right to know, now. To make plans.'* Then she slugged down a shot."

Phil let out a long, slow breath. "Christ."

"Yeah. He died in his thirties, too."

Phil struggled for something encouraging to say. "Well, but, you were never like him, Jason. You didn't take after him."

"Jesus?"

"Funny. No, I mean your father. Did you ever have a cardiologist check you out?"

"Yeah. Three. They ran all the tests."

"And?"

"They didn't find anything wrong. They said I was strong as a horse."

"Well there you go! You probably take after your mother's side of the family."

"Maybe."

"Probably. How old was your mother's father when he died?"

"Early forties."

"Aw crap, Jason. Are you kidding me?"

"No. He fell off a horse."

—10—

The Acid Reflux was crowded with hungry diners when Jason and Phil came in out of a drizzly rain. Once again their nostrils filled with the aromas of great food, rolled in batter and deep fried to greasy, crunchy perfection.

Phil angled toward the back of the restaurant while Jason inspected plates of golden fish sticks with fries and fried chicken with fries and mounds of plump, overcooked spaghetti coated in tomato sauce, with fries. Cheap, tasty food loaded with carbs to fill the belly and comfort the soul. Red plastic placemats had been added to the tables, with silverware rolled up inside paper napkins. Phil had said they fancied things up for dinner.

They found a table in the middle of the noise, close to a 1950s jukebox, rainbow colors spilling across the front grill, Waylon Jennings, the outlaw, singing to the choir. The diners ate mostly in silence, absorbing every word.

Louie approached the table with a paper towel folded over his arm. He handed Jason a one-sided menu. "The special this evening is French fries."

"Anything else?" Jason asked.

"On a plate."

"Diet cokes okay?" Phil asked Jason. "Bring us a couple, will you, Louie? And how about some bread sticks and butter."

"You need a few minutes to order?" Louie asked.

"The fish sticks are very good," Phil said to Jason. "Real fillets, not the minced. That's what I'm having."

"Yeah, okay." Jason handed the menu back to Louie. "I hope it comes with the evening special. And a dill pickle."

"I can pin it on you if you want. Then we'll all know you have one." Louie shuffled away, grumbling under his breath.

"He doesn't like me," Jason said. "I can tell. Don't ask me how."

"You ask for it."

"Maybe."

"Louie's all right. He treats almost everybody the same, except the Bananas. And pedophiles. Won't let them in the door."

"He owns the place?"

"Won it in a poker game about twenty years ago. It was vacant, boarded up, worth shit. He was in a car wreck, somebody ran a red light and T-boned the passenger side, killed his wife, smashed him up pretty bad. He got a lousy settlement, lousy lawyer, but enough to sink into this place. He lives alone upstairs, no family."

"Who does the cooking? He can't pay much."

"A couple illegals. They live someplace in the building. They get three squares plus minimum. There's not much chance they'll get caught, at work anyway. The Bananas won't eat in here. They're afraid, rightly, somebody will poison their food."

Jason's stomach rumbled. The smells were incredible, like walking through a corridor of food vendors at a county fair back in the nostalgic days, not long ago, when America still was. "I could swear I smell kettle corn."

"You do. It's the house special dessert. Or fried apple pie."

Jason watched the smoky parade of hoopties and Banana military vehicles prowling Twine Street, no particular hurry, just cruising the anarchy and mayhem timeslot, windshield wipers swatting gloomy rain. He checked his watch. They had plenty of time to get back to Phil's office before dark. A vagrant stopped now and then, peered inside at the diners, then slowly ambled on.

"Where do the homeless sleep at night?" Jason asked. "The ones who can't afford the Hot L? I didn't see any on the street when I got here this morning."

"Usually the nooks and crannies around the railroad yard, empty warehouses. If it gets real cold they'll crawl down through a storm drain into the tunnels. I don't ask. The homeless shelters are packed so they have to fend for themselves. They're very protective, very secretive about their hiding places. Somebody'll steal it, or rob them, or the Bananas will root them out for the fun of it. *Bumming*, they call it. It's the latest hunting sport."

Louie arrived with a basket of hard bread sticks and a small dish of cold butter cubes individually wrapped in foil. Phil dumped them out and began patiently picking off the foil, dropping the peeled cubes into the dish. "How many homeless would you guess are in Seattle?"

Jason chomped off the end of a breadstick. "I don't know. A thousand?"

"It was about nine thousand before Trump's putsch. New York has the highest number. Incredible underground system there. Kansas City and Vegas have a lot of mole people in their tunnels. How many would you guess were spread around the country before the shit hit?"

Jason shrugged.

"About six-hundred thousand," Phil said. "As of a few months ago. I don't know what the numbers are now. A lot of veterans. Thousands in tent cities, tens of thousands living in their cars. That doubled when Trump cut billions out of healthcare—and I

161

mean billions and billions. Research, too, that took a big hit. Aid for the poor was cut in half. When he frocked himself it was cut to zero. He's gutted everything. No more poor problem if there are no more poor. The regime doesn't care. They don't live anywhere near places like here."

"A lot of them are mentally ill, aren't they?"

"The regime? I think morally bankrupt is more accurate."

"I like *debauched*. I meant the homeless, though; a lot of them are mentally ill."

"It's all changing. There's a lot more destitute now. It used to be about a third. Most are harmless. They just need their meds. When they started closing down the big institutions in the eighties, the promise was they'd set up neighborhood clinics so people could get treatment and help—cheap housing, a job they could handle, a *life*. Didn't happen. They dumped them out on the streets and the patients were too confused to know what they were supposed to do. So, they self-medicate with bum wine— Thunderbird, Night Train, made by Gallo, by the way, but they won't put their name on the label. If you like the smell of your hands after pumping gas, you'll love this stuff. It's foul crap but their taste-buds are shot and they can get numb in a hurry. Wherever you see pigeon shit you'll find the empty bottles. It's a five hundred-million-dollar misery market, skid-row fortified wines like Wild Irish

162

Rose, cheap ingredients and lots of sugar and alcohol so they won't feel as hungry, with a few drops of grape juice."

"The institutions were like snake-pit places though, weren't they?" Jason asked.

"A few were pretty bad. Mostly they didn't have the staff to handle all the patients, so they over-medicated or put them in isolation. Calling the hospitals 'lunatic asylums' didn't help. Mental illness is in the same category leprosy used to be. Families are embarrassed to talk about it. It's not a respectable disease like cancer and diabetes."

Phil stabbed a cold butter cube with a skinny breadstick and crunched several seconds. "Here's a little experiment for you. The next time you're sitting around with a group of friends or whoever, and one of them says their husband is having prostate surgery and somebody else says their mother is on kidney dialysis or some such, listen to the sympathy they get, then casually drop in something like, your brother is being treated for manic depression. Watch the reaction. You ever sprinkle water on popcorn?"

"Why would I do that?"

"It instantly shrivels up. It's the same reaction with people. It's embarrassing to watch, the first time; after that it's interesting. There are surprises. The funny thing is, most of them probably have family members with the same thing but they'd never admit it."

163

Jason watched him closely. "Is this personal?"

"Oh-ho. Yeah. Very personal. Fucking personal. The government swept them out the door, down the streets, into the alleys, under the bridges. They're sent to jail, treated like major criminals for minor shit, like blacks are treated. When they get out they just want to find a dry hole to live in. The families don't know what to do, where to go for help." Louie had approached and stood close behind Phil, listening.

"A lot of patients have never been heard from again. My brother was in and out of a state hospital, actually the same place where 'Cuckoo's Nest' was filmed."

"Wow. Was he one of the characters they portrayed? Jack Nicholson? Danny DeVito?" Phil turned a cold stare on him. Jason hung his head. "Sorry."

"Garner had mild schizophrenia, only a problem if he went off his meds. He'd take it, feel better and think he didn't need it anymore. My folks always went to visit, every visiting day. One day they went and they were told he'd been released. They asked where? When? Days ago, they were told. They asked why they weren't told, so they could come and pick him up. No answer. Didn't know, didn't care. They spent weeks searching the streets for him. They found him once but didn't know who to call to help get him back on his meds. He disappeared again.

That was about twenty-five years ago. We have no idea if he's dead or alive." Phil broke a bread stick in half and jabbed another butter cube. "So yes, it's personal."

"Cheerful dinner discussion," Louie said. "I suppose you're going to blame my food if it don't sit right."

"No," Phil said. "I'll blame Jason here."

"Yeah, I would," Louie said. "How about some evening entertainment?"

"Am I it?" Jason said dryly.

"No. This is actually entertaining." Louie pulled over an empty chair, sat down and folded his hairy arms on the table. "A lawyer dies and meets Saint Peter and Gabriel standing outside the Pearly Gates. *'Give me one good reason,'* Peter says, *'why I should let you in?'* And the lawyer says, *'Just a week ago I gave a quarter to a homeless guy layin' on the street.'* So Peter checks with Gabriel and he says, *'Yep, there it is, the big twenty-five cent donation.'* Peter shakes his head no, like, you gotta be kidding me.

"So, the lawyer panics and says, *'Wait, there's more! A couple years ago I gave a quarter to another homeless guy.'* So, Peter checks with Gabriel and yeah, it's true. Peter gets in a huddle with Gabriel and asks what he should do with this guy. Gabriel gives the lawyer a long look and says, *'Give him back his fifty cents and tell him to go to hell.'*"

165

Louie looked pleased when they laughed. "Okay now," he said, standing up. "Knock off the depressing shit while you're having your dinner. You got all night to talk about it."

They sat double-dipping and crunching on breadsticks while the Everly Brothers harmonized on the jukebox. Louie brought their dinners, on white ceramic plates.

"Do you have tartar sauce?" Jason asked.

Louie pointed to the ketchup bottle.

"That's ketchup," Jason said.

"Very good. And that's a fork, and that's a knife, the black stuff there is pepper, the white stuff is salt. Enjoy your dinner." He turned to leave, then glanced back. "You want kettle corn for dessert?"

"Yeah, to go. Thanks, Louie."

Jason squeezed a mound of ketchup on the side of his plate. "We're not coming here for breakfast, are we?"

"No. You'll need to make the moment last."

Jason took a bite of the fish stick. It was very good, tender and flakey. He felt his mood improve with every bite. "What's your wife like?" he asked.

"A jewel. Beautiful voice. She performs in local playhouses. She eats too much salt. Loves butter. Loves looking for UFOs."

"So do I. She ever see any?"

"Two positive sightings. The first was two erratic zips around the sky, lasted a couple minutes,

166

too fast and zig-zaggy to be anything from our planet. The second one was like half a glowing ball, bottom half, moving slow across the sky. She's convinced it has something to do with her apple."

"Her computer?"

"No. An apple. A real apple. The same night she saw the lighted dome, she says there was an apple out on the deck table. The next morning, it was gone. She's been putting one out every night since. Every morning, it's gone. She likes to think it's friendly banter between our two worlds."

"Kids, probably."

"Tall kids. We live on the ninth floor."

"Who do you think's taking them?"

"I don't know. I'm thinking more *what* than *who*. Probably a large bird. Maybe a squirrel."

"Yeah, probably. If the aliens wanted apples, why not just go pick them off a tree? Beam up a bushel. They could do all the experiments they want, try to figure out how apples have sex, make baby apples. Put two of them in some hay and see if they have a roll."

Phil snickered.

"I wonder how aliens have sex," Jason went on. "They never have genitals in the movies. They did a biopsy on that dead one that crashed in Roswell and there were no visible sex organs."

"Hoax."

"Maybe, but they wanted it to look real and the aliens' jewels have to be tucked away someplace. If the hoaxers went to the trouble of using sheep brains in raspberry jam and knuckle joints and chicken entrails to make it look authentic, why not make some silicone alien version of a penis or vagina?"

"Jesus H. Christ," Louie muttered as he refilled their drink glasses. "How you guys can eat, I'll never know. Did you ever hear of good dinner conversation?"

"What does the 'H' stand for?" Jason said.

"Harold. You know, 'Our Father, who art in heaven, Harold be thy name.'"

"I thought it stood for . . ." Jason started to say. He stopped, listening. "That's a pretty big truck to be coming down this street isn't it?" He felt a slight swaying motion, then the floor began to shake, the dishes clattering on the tabletops, the shuddering vibrations intensifying as the sound, like an eighteen-wheeler, roared closer. The other diners continued eating, unperturbed. "Earthquake?" Jason asked.

Louie shook his head. "Trump's Tower Tank. He's testing it here. It's about two stories high, the most ridiculous contraption you ever saw. Gotta be the biggest, tallest, greatest armored vehicle ever. Slow as hell but nothing's stopped it so far—rockets, grenades, whatever the Bananas shoot at it. Trump wants it perfect before the next parade. And gold-plated, the big *tah-dah!* when he steps out and waves to his masses of fans.   Masses his asses. They're ordered there or they're shot. Whatta guy. Whatta show."

"That still next month?" Phil said.

"Far as I know. They're scrambling to get the Trump logo painted in big letters on all the missiles and bombs. The NRA is pissed. They want their logo on at least the big bullets."

The violent shaking and noise rose to a crescendo as the massive object labored past the front windows, blocking out the light.

"My back teeth are chattering," Jason said.

"Clinch them," Phil said.

The room grew dark and no one spoke until a sliver of daylight appeared and slowly spread across the diner. Trump's Tower Tank gradually crawled on its fat belly down the street."

"How many does it hold?" Jason asked.

"Two. By the time it was fitted with a luxury bathroom and upstairs bedroom, they could only squeeze in two Bananas. It's all for looks. Intimidation. Trump's bully tank."

Louie sat down. "Gonna be here for the pledge tomorrow?" he asked Jason.

"What's that?"

"A very moving moment. Every morning at dawn, everyone has to stand facing Mar-a-Lago and say the Pledge of Loyalty, hand over your crotch."

Jason was horrified. "Fuck that!"

Louie cackled. "I like this one, Phil. He's so easy to bait." He tapped his thick fingers on the table, scrutinizing Jason. "Phil tell you about MUSCLE?"

"Yeah."

"Interested?"

"Yeah."

"Know where the Shithole building is?"

"No."

"Good." He lowered his voice. "I want you to listen to me, now. Sometime after tomorrow, when your shit's done with Phil, come back here to Twine and look for a green door. It's the only green door for blocks so you can't miss it unless you're color-blind. Are you?"

"No."

"Go in, go up to the third floor and look for another green door. Knock one time. That's it. Once. When a guy opens the door, ask for Laszlo."

"Who's Laszlo?"

"You don't need to know that now. Are you going to remember what I'm telling you? You're sitting there looking stupid at me.

"I heard you. Green door. Two knocks. Laszlo."

"I just got done sayin'—!

"I like this one, Phil," Jason interrupted. "He's so easy to bait."

"Yeah, well, we'll see if you show up, funny guy." Louie stood to leave. "You know what the moral of all this is?"

"I give up," Jason replied dryly.

"Enjoy your kettle corn."

"What?"

"Enjoy your kettle corn." He turned to Phil. "If you want fried pie, too, let me know."

When Louie was out of earshot, Jason said, "I don't know how to take him."

"He's resistance. He likes you, Jason. If he didn't, he wouldn't say a word. I had one client, Louie *accidently* spilled ice water on his lap." Phil started to chuckle. "Louie says, '*I'm sorry. I thought you were another asshole.*'"

Jason stared out at the darkening street, looking scarier by the minute. "What are those flashing lights?"

"I don't know. I'm not out there."

"Maybe my life's starting to flash before my eyes. I go out that door and boom, I meet my maker." He put a two-dollar tip on the table. "Just my luck it'll be my father."

—11—

Drake was waiting for them on the wet sidewalk next to Jason's Prius.

"Something's wrong," Phil said. "He shouldn't be here now. He goes behind the diner to eat this time of day." He opened the stairwell door and started inside. "You wait here."

Jason tried not to panic as he glanced up and down the foreboding street. The gangs were gathering in ominous clusters, some staring at him. A huge bonfire crackled, shooting flames and sparks high into the air. Herman's saxophone wailed in the darkening hellhole "You're going to leave me out here on the street alone?" Jason squawked.

"Do you want to come with me?"

"No! I say fuck it and let's go get a drink."

"I'll be right back."

Jason shoved his hands in his pockets and casually backed himself against the building, trying to look relaxed, cool, laid back. His eyes darted left to right, on high alert for any suspicious movement

172

gravitating his direction. He broke into a heart-hammering cold sweat.

"Nice bird," he cooed nicely to Drake. "Did you see a bad thing in there? Did someone get slaughtered in the stairwell and there's blood and guts all over the walls? Why are you walking away?" He whistled softly. "Here, bird. Drake! Come back, boy. You work for Phil, remember? That means you work for me, too." By some miracle Drake waddled back and stood next to him, his head jerking this way and that, observing, scrutinizing, like a bodyguard.

"You packing heat?" Jason said, working to calm himself. "Got a Taser under your wing there, buddy?"

His breath became shorter and faster, his ears felt plugged; his knees began to tremble as the seconds dragged on. Subwoofers in the trunks of passing cars *thumpathumpathumped* deep inside his chest. "Oh fuck shit and hell," he muttered, "I'm going to die." He felt vomit rising in his throat.

The stairwell door opened. "You can come in now," Phil said.

Jason flung the door open and barreled past him. "What took you so long! What was it?"

"You're going to see some drops of blood going up the stairs, past my door. They go on up to Carly's place. But don't worry about it."

"Who's Carly?"

173

"Bed and Beaver. Third floor. Everything's all right."

"How can it be all right if somebody's bleeding out in your building?"

"They're not bleeding out. I said drops of blood, not pools." He started upstairs. "It's all right. Come on. If she needs help, she'll ask."

Jason carefully avoided the blood spatters on the steps, a lot more than drops, but not pools, not pools. None on the walls. Whose blood was it, he wondered. A woman? A man? Were they shot? Knifed? Were they dying, right this very minute, in some squalid hole over his head? He followed Phil into the office and swiftly shut the door.

"How can you be so calm?"

Phil removed his hat and deftly tossed it onto the coatrack. "I pace myself."

"They could be dying."

"He isn't."

"You know it's a man?"

"Who was stabbed in the shoulder, a shallow wound, and the bleeding has stopped, and he's probably getting laid as we speak. Carly will make him feel all better, all right?"

Jason shrugged. "I guess it happens all the time around here. I almost pissed my pants."

Phil nodded toward the bathroom door. When Jason came out, Phil was pouring a bag of Louie's kettle corn into a bowl. "Feeling better now?" He set the bowl in the center of the desk and gave the banker's lamp chain a quick yank. The grass-green shade glowed warm and spilled soft light into the dusky room.

Jason sat down and rubbed his aching knees. "Does anybody ever bother calling the cops?"

"We don't have cops anymore, remember? We have Banana Enforcers. And no, nobody calls them."

"What happens if somebody's shot?"

"They bleed."

"You mean, there's nobody who stops the shooters?"

Phil shrugged.

"They could stand on the street and shoot out your windows and there's nothing you could do?"

"Calm down, Jason. I get along with the people here. None of them are going to shoot my windows, or my clients, or your car, unless you do something stupid to piss them off. The Bananas are too busy trying to keep themselves from getting shot. If you haven't noticed, they're hated here."

"But there are a lot of shootings here, right? This used to be called the Crosshairs District for a reason."

"A lot of guns are sold here. There are the usual drive-bys and gang fights. Somebody might lob a missile. If it hits the roof we're okay, we're two stories down. We're going to stay inside until tomorrow morning, so don't worry about it."

Jason leaned back and tried to relax. It was completely dark outside now. Reflections from the bonfire flames danced brighter on the window. Drake and another pigeon had hunkered down on the ledge, heads tucked under their wings. "Is that other bird his mate?"

"Yes. They mate for life. They do it better than we do. Some screw around but they always come back. As far as I know, Drake's been faithful to her."

"How did you get this relationship you have with him? I swear, he understood every word I said out on the street."

"I found him about four years ago, tangled up in a plastic six-pack ring out on the sidewalk by the door. He didn't have any choice but let me help him. I brought him up here and cut him loose, then put him out on the ledge there. He was still there when I went to lunch. Louie had some stale bread and when I got back he was still there. I fed him some crumbs and . . . we've been pals ever since."

"Smart."

"Actually, yes. Pigeons are as good at math as rhesus monkeys, and they can be trained to do almost any task, like monkeys. Also, most interestingly, they recognize people. If someone is mean to them, they never forget it. Even if the person tries to be nice the next time, too late. Drake knows everybody around here. He knew you were a stranger this morning."

"You were watching?"

"Yes."

"Did you laugh?"

"Yes."

"Did you know I gave him the finger?"

"That's all right. He cut you some slack."

"Did you hear that scream just now?"

"Vaguely. I tune most of it out."

"It sounded close. I can't believe we can't call the cops anymore."

"Did you call them very often?"

"No. I don't think I ever did."

"Ever have any run-ins?"

"No."

"Never questioned? No? That's pretty amazing."

"Why?"

"Most of us have been stopped for one reason or another—speeding, running a light." Phil was fishing for the stop-and-frisk incident.

"Oh yeah, I was questioned once. Kind of. Maybe almost arrested. Amy said they were ready to cuff me. I don't think it went that far."

"She was with you?"

"We were in the car heading up to Anacortes, catch the ferry over to Friday Harbor. We were kind of half disagreeing, half talking, just having a good conversation, I thought.

177

"Are we going to talk about the emoluments clause the entire trip?" she asked in a pleasant, warning tone.

"No. I'm just trying to keep the conversation interesting."

"And what I'm talking about is boring?"

"No! You said you were worried about profits at the bakery and I was just elaborating, adding to what you said."

"I know what elaborating means."

"Elaborating with interesting information."

"About Trump. Again. I was talking about our earnings going down."

"Yes. And I was adding that Trump's making big profits being president and maybe your family should follow our leader. Sell merchandise stamped with Mcfine's Bakery with a motto like, 'Make America Gluten Again,' since you make a lot of bread—you know, some funny twist like that. You could put it on more than caps. He sells all kinds of stuff—dog collars, mugs, coolies, Christmas ornaments. You could put a little string of battery lights on the caps and double the price like he did. Really great deals."

"Really not funny." She frowned out the window.

"Too bad you can't take a vacation every weekend and charge your customers. If you built some McFine hotels you could herd all your out-of-

town visitors into them and sell McFine Wine. If you owned some golf-courses . . . wait, here's an idea. You could park luxury pay-to-pee porta-potties along the waterfront and charge them off. If somebody sues you for illegal parking, the customers—we the customers of the United States — we'd have to pay all the attorney fees." He grinned. "This is getting better by the minute. Who knew profiteering could be so rich with possibilities? We could . . ."

"We can go back home. That's what we can do." Her face was tight. He shut up.

They rode for several minutes in a heavy thrum of traffic heading north on Interstate 5. Mount Baker loomed high over the Cascade Range to the east, shimmering in a cloak of ice and hardened snow. He could feel the chill in the car.

"That was a good movie last night," he said. She said nothing. "What was it called again? The Lake House? Yeah, that was something, him living in a house she lived in two years before and they're in a time warp thing. I liked the parts showing the mailbox flopping open and closed. Flopping open. Flopping closed. I'm glad the red flag went up in time. That was a close one. I'm glad we watched it again."

He was lying through his teeth. His brain squeezed ether into his eyeballs the entire, interminable, ninety-eight minutes. He liked the

179

ending, when the two long-suffering lovers finally meet and Amy cried and he held her and comforted her and walked her tenderly into bed.

"You're driving too fast," she said.

"I'm going with the flow," he said. "The eighty-fifth percentile speed, the speed eighty-five out of a hundred cars are traveling. I'm not passing anybody."

"Okay," she sang, not believing.

"Did I tell you how beautiful you look today?"

She smiled. "Just today?"

"You're always gorgeous. Today you are especially magnificent and luscious."

"Just watch the road." She smiled over at him, the dimples deepening in her velvet cheeks, her eyes soft and sparkling and lovely.

For the millionth time he asked himself how he got so lucky. "Did you ever hear from Mel again? Mel Stiner?"

"He called once. I told him I was in a relationship. I don't think he'll call again. Did you ever call the cable company about the bill?"

"I'm still trying to find an email address. All I'm getting is CHAT pop-ups. I don't want to chat. I want it in writing."

"You never talked to anybody?"

"Yes. I talked to ten somebodies. They all said something different. They all said they would fix it. They all said there was no record I'd called them

before. I told them I'd talked to Tom and Kim and George and Bill and Betty. That's very strange, they said, because there's nothing in the file that I'd called before. Like I'm lying. That's why I want to email, to have something in writing. But they don't have emails anymore. They have Chats, so they can say anything they want and there's no written record and they can sit in their boiler rooms and laugh their asses off because it's so easy to screw the customer if you're stuck in a contract.

"If Russia cuts our internet cables, we'll get the bill. That's just part of normal service now. Russia's hacking into everything—airlines, water, electrical grids, nuclear. All those glitches here and there, they're just testing it out till they're ready for the big blow. What's Trump doing? Nothing. 'You're a bad boy, Putin. Go to my room.' What's congress doing? Nothing. Are we able to hack into their systems? Is anybody working on that? Who knows? Nobody talks about it."

"Please slow down."

He eased off the gas pedal. "Tomorrow I'm going to write a letter to their corporate office and tell them I'm going to complain to my congressman." He snorted a laugh. "Yeah right. They probably contributed to his PAC. Did you know politicians actually ask lobbyists to have fundraisers for their campaigns? They are

181

spectacularly worthless, bought and paid for by the NRA, Wall Street, Big Pharma—"

"Oh please, Jason, enough! Can't we have even one nice day?"

"We can talk about corruption and still have a nice day. I just want you to understand where I'm coming from."

"I understand you enough. I don't want to understand any more. I don't want to be as miserable as you. Dammit Jason, you're tail-gating that car."

"Okay, yes, I see it. I'm just saying, I'm tired of being somebody's bottom line. 'We can't insure you because, bottom line, there's no profit.' 'We can't remove your spleen because, bottom line, there's no profit.'"

"Why would they need to remove your spleen?"

"It could herniate. It's rare, but it happens. They won't pay for experimental procedures. That's the only kind I get. If they save me, I'll just cost them more money down the line so, bottom line, let me die. It's a total win-win for them."

"Jason—"

"I feel like that big rump roast those two fishermen in Jaws threw into the ocean as bait. That's what I am, that's what we all are, just dead meat dragging the bottom line of life. Shark food."

"Will you please, please slow down?"

"The faster we get there, the less time there is to have an accident."

"That makes no sense. Speeders have more accidents than law-abiding drivers."

"Not true. They get arrested more. And if they're in an accident they're more likely to die from the high-speed impact, but if they're not, they get where they're going a lot sooner and greatly reduce their time on dangerous highways."

"Made even more dangerous by speeding lawbreakers who talk too much and forget where they are and lose control and take innocent drivers—and passengers— out with them."

He shrugged. "That's one way to look at it. I would just rather get where we're going as soon as possible and avoid risks that involve injuries. One-hundred percent of all injuries are painful, Amy, unless they happen to somebody else. Or you're unconscious. I'd fly more often but what's the point? The airlines don't let you take survival gear."

"You never fly anywhere."

"I want to. I will, when they let me carry on survival gear. They're charging to carry on wallets, now."

"You can check in gear. Most reasonable gear."

"What good is survival gear stuffed into a cargo hold? You have to have time to strap it on."

She rubbed a headache that was beginning to squeeze her forehead. "So, like, the plane cracks open like an egg in the middle of the sky, and you have time to parachute out? Is that the plan?"

"Not a parachute. I said survival gear—a tent, water purifiers, fire starters, signaling gear, shark repellent—or something that can kill a shark if it gets too close, say, within a mile. The odor from a dead shark repels live sharks, some chemical their glands release when—"

"Oh, for god's sake, shut up! Shut up-shut up-shut up! Or stop the car and let me out right now. Just stop the car. Stop the car, Jason. Right now. Pull over."

"I can't pull over. A semi is on our ass."

"Then slow down and let him pass, then pull over."

"I can't change speed right now, Amy. We're in a semi sandwich." The back end of a mammoth, snarling Freightliner filled the windshield.

She glared straight ahead, her hands gripped into tight fists on her lap, tears flowing without a sound.

"Oh god, Amy, I'm sorry. I'm sorry! I was just blabbing, just talking to pass the time. I won't say another word till we get there. I promise."

"I want to go home."

"Come on, Amy. We're almost there. An hour from now we'll be cruising toward Friday Harbor,

Vinny's Ristorante, drunken manila clams, lasagna." She didn't blink. "Mi dispiace," he said softly. "TI amo, Amy. IO sono una merda."

"What's the last one."

"I'm a shit."

She shook her head. "You're an asshole. You have lost it, Jason, do you know that? Don't answer. Just . . . please, don't say anything until I signal you with my finger—this finger, Jason—then you can speak. The sound of your voice is eating like acid through my brain. It's crackling inside my skull. I can't stand it another second! If you utter one sound before the signal I'm going to open the door and jump out. I mean it! Just . . . drive."

He gripped the wheel and they rode in rigid silence. He thought of apologizing again and started to open his mouth. Her head whipped in his direction and fired a ballistic glare. He gulped and shrank down in the seat.

How did he let himself get into this dangerous situation again? No matter how many times his stupidity gored the relationship, over and over again he put on the red scarf and sash, stood on a cobbled street in Pamplona, a rocket was shot and the running of his mouth began. He was so busy racing and strategizing and covering ground he never saw the approaching Toro Bravo horns until the slobber was in his back pocket and he was flung over the fence.

185

He gradually eased off the gas. The semi behind them fell back, then roared around and passed. The empty space widened several comfortable car-lengths ahead of them. After another tense ten miles of silence, Amy lifted the finger into the air but said nothing.

"We're almost out of Snohomish County," he offered meekly. "Yeah, there's the sign, we're entering Skagit County."

He increased his speed in anticipation of the turn-off a few miles ahead. Twelve miles after that they would arrive at the ferry entrance to the San Juan Islands. Luckily, he'd been able to secure a reservation on the next crossing. All he wanted to do was get her on the ferry, hold her close, and put this ridiculous argument behind them.

The sky was brilliant blue, the air like wine. He whipped around a crawling RV with Montana plates and sailed full steam ahead, down to the sea with ships! They would snuggle together, he and his Amy, destined soulmates, and watch the evergreen hills and fertile valleys slide by, past old smuggler's beaches and tranquil bays, into deep harbors and out again, slicing the frigid waters of the Salish Sea into effervescent sheaves.

Only one-hundred and twenty-eight of the four-hundred plus islands were named, only four of these accessible by Washington State ferries. Morning to midnight they plied the protected

186

waters between the US mainland and Canada as deftly as orcas and gray and minke and humpback whales.

"We've got it all, Amy," he almost sang. "We've got it all!"

"You've got State Troopers, Jason. Look in the rearview."

His heart seized when he saw the flashing blue lights. It jumped and dropped like a dead fish in his chest when a siren whooped a warning, then whooped again. Jason flipped the right turn-signal and eased onto the far-right side of the highway. He lowered his window clear down, turned off the ignition and put the keys on the dashboard so they would know he wasn't an escape risk. He gripped the steering wheel with both hands and watched the white patrol car in the rear-view mirror pull in behind him.

"Is he getting out?" Amy whispered.

"No. He's just sitting there. He's probably reporting he has us stopped, checking out the license plate. He's getting out now! Shit-shit-shit!"

"Calm down, Jason. This isn't a manhunt."

"Good morning, sir." A young trooper with red hair and freckles showed his badge. His name was Martin Miller. His face was pleasant. Jason relaxed. "Could I see your license and registration, please? Just take it out of your wallet, sir." While he studied it, Jason leaned over and retrieved the

insurance and registration envelope from the glove box and handed it over.

Another trooper, the partner, had ambled over and stood like a stocky bulldog a few feet behind trooper Miller, hands on his hips, blue uniform crisp with authority. He wasn't nearly as friendly looking. His gun looked meaner than Martin's.

"Do you know why I pulled you over?" trooper Miller asked.

"No."

"Do you know what the speed limit is on this portion of the highway?"

Jason thought quickly. "Eighty."

"Do you know how fast you were driving before I pulled you over?"

"Uh, I'm not sure. I think maybe eighty-one."

"Plus five. You were driving eighty-six miles an hour. Your speed has been erratic. Is this an emergency situation, sir? Are you or your passenger in need of immediate medical care?"

Amy hugged her arms and stared at the floor.

"No," Jason said nervously. "There's no emergency. Excuse me, but . . . could you move a little bit more to your left?"

Trooper Miller stiffened and stared hard at him. "Excuse me, sir?"

"Just a few inches?" Jason flicked his fingers a couple inches to his right, directing the trooper in

the direction Jason thought he should move. "I don't think your body camera is aimed toward me." He smiled and shrugged. "I know, I'm not black, but I'd feel more comfortable."

Amy covered her face with her hands. "This isn't happening," she whispered.

Trooper Miller stepped back, away from the door. He no longer looked friendly. "I need you to slowly step out of the vehicle. Do not make any sudden moves."

The partner fixed a dangerous glare on Jason and took two giant steps forward.

Jason opened the car door. "I just want to be sure the camera picks up everything." He eased out of the car, trying to breathe normally. "I didn't want half the video to be the steering wheel and windshield if this goes viral."

Trooper Miller stared at Jason's slacks. "Are you carrying a weapon?"

"No. Sir."

"What is that in your right pocket?"

"What? Oh. It's a harmonica."

"That's a new one," the partner grumbled.

"I need you to slowly turn around and place your feet shoulder-width apart. Lean forward and place your open hands a foot apart on the roof of the car."

Trooper Miller patted him down to the bulge in his pants pocket, removed the harmonica, and finished the pat search. "Just a harmonica," he told his partner. He handed it over.

The partner turned it this way and that, then smirked. "You play this thing?"

"No," Jason replied.

"Why do you carry it, then?"

Jason thought frantically. Truth or lie? "Because it looks like a weapon. I don't believe in carrying a gun. My hands are my weapons. And my feet."

The bulldog laughed heartily. Jason felt weak and needed to sit.

"All right," trooper Miller said. "You can get back in the car." He handed the harmonica and documents back to Jason. "I'm not going to issue you a citation this time. But I want you to think about this. You are right about one thing. That appendage on the end of your leg is a weapon when it's on a gas pedal. This highway isn't a NASCAR track." Jason hung his head and listened solemnly, respectfully, to the entire lecture.

When it was finished, there was a moment of silence. Jason nodded that he thoroughly agreed but felt compelled to respond. "I'm more likely to die from a gun than a car crash, though."

Trooper Miller quirked his head. "What?"

"In seventeen states, including Washington, I'm more likely to die from a gun than a car wreck. Probably the reason the number of car accidents is *reducing is because there are fewer drivers because they're getting shot."*

"What is your point, Mr. Nickle? That since you believe you will die from a gunshot, you are going to continue to drive fast in the meantime?"

"No. It was just an observation." He'd blown it again. He saw Amy imperceptivity shake her head and stare out the window, away from him.

"Here is my observation," trooper Miller said. "I am going to be watching for this vehicle every time I am on duty. If I catch you speeding again, you are going to be playing that harmonica in a jail cell. I should probably go ahead and just ticket you now."

"I think he needs a ticket," the partner growled. "I don't think he heard a word you said. I think we've got a smart-ass here."

"No, no, I heard you. I'm really sorry I was speeding. I've just been upset lately about all the gun violence. I understand the consequences of driving too fast and I'll slow down immediately, from now on. I really do appreciate the opportunity to correct my driving mistake before anything serious happens. A safe driving record is very important to me."

The partner frowned, sniffed and eyeballed the passing traffic easing by, well under the speed limit.

191

The troopers returned to their car and sat watching as Jason turned on his left blinkers, waited for a wide break in traffic, and slowly eased back onto the highway. Seconds later the patrol car pulled up behind him and followed for what seemed like several miles. It finally pulled out and passed. Jason wondered if he should smile and wave. He decided against it and concentrated on the speed gauge.

"You never learn, do you," Amy said at last. "You just have to say whatever pops into your head."

"I was just trying to make a point."

"Oh I know. I just wish they'd taken you to jail."

—12—

Close to midnight, Herman's forlorn saxophone became a haunting, plaintive wail, invisible ribbons curling into dark doorways and alleys, past lurking predators and jaded victims who stayed anyway. Discordant cries and shouts penetrating the closed office window were several decibels louder, a clattering distant train sounding much closer, as though hurtling headlong up the street.

Jason wanted to peer out and see how Twine Street looked at the peak of anarchy and mayhem, but he'd be an easy target, an easy shot, backlit by the banker's lamp.

"Does Herman play every night?" he asked Phil. They were stretched out in their leather chairs, munching kettle corn.

"Just about. His legs were crushed in a logging accident, some fly-by-night company. No insurance. He gets around on two canes. Bad arthritis. He's one of the free-loaders Trump and his cronies threw off disability."

"Trump said he had jobs for a lot of them. The 'obvious cripples' could take phone reservations at his resorts. The bedridden could be internet cops. Great guy. Heart of fool's gold." He closed his eyes and listened to the music. "Can Herman get a job playing in a club? He's good."

"He can't read music. He basically plays variations of the same song." Phil crunched a few more caramelized kernels. "So, anything more you want to say about American terrorists?" He had been carefully maneuvering the conversation all evening, backtracking, rehashing.

"No, except they're not called terrorists if they're white. They're lone-wolf gunmen or troubled young bombers. You have to be one of fifty shades of brown to be called a terrorist. Remember the good old days of Al Capone, Bonnie and Clyde, Bugsy Siegel?"

"No. I wasn't born yet."

"I mean, thinking back when we knew who the bad guys were. Crime back then was ours. We owned it. Good ol' American bank robberies, prostitution, gambling, the rackets, spiffed up dudes in silk suits and greasy hair and diamond rings, sexy broads to slap around. It was all about greed, money, power. When they killed each other, it was mostly business. Line up your rivals in a garage and mow 'em down, jump out of a cake with a machine gun, blast some Sicilian's face off while they're eating spaghetti. We knew how they operated. We knew how to end them." He shook his head. "The terrorists, they're like they're not even . . . human. Do you believe in the concept of evil?"

"I believe some people do evil things. Things like the Holocaust, nerve gas—the word *'wrong'* doesn't cut it." Phil glanced uneasily at his watch. With so much left to cover, there really wasn't time for philosophical discussions. "When you —"

"So, you don't believe in supernatural evil forces?" Jason asked.

"I'm not sure. What gets into two ten-year-old kids to brutally murder a two-year-old? I don't know if we'll ever know, not in this life anyway. Do you believe in a Satan or Lucifer?"

"Let's just say, I would never call the devil 'Beelzebub' to his face."

"Are you religious, Jason?"

Jason winced. "That word makes my testicles cringe. I'm not kidding. I have a charley-horse in my balls." He crossed his legs and shifted position. "If you're asking if I believe in God, yes, because he isn't religious—he doesn't turn the screws on voters, doesn't knock people on their ass when he heals them. Actually, the word 'religion' is almost meaningless. Google it. You'll get over seven-hundred thousand sects, cults, schisms, isms, hisms, hersms. There'd be a lot more, but they kill each other. Look at the Bananas, riding around on their trucks, index fingers in the air, laughing and loving it because people are terrified of them. They got that from watching ISIS."

"What does that mean, the index finger?"

"The only true religion. World dominance. That's Trump's plan. You think he wants to stop with this country? He wants it all."

Jason smirked, lost in thought. "I had a huge fight one time with my father, the first time I ever saw him turn purple. He went ballistic when I said Jesus wasn't white. I asked him how he could think anything else? Jesus was a Middle-Eastern Jew. He looked like every other brown-skinned Israelite. If he didn't, all Judas would have had to do was lead the soldiers to the Garden and say, '*That's him over there, the white guy.*'"

Phil chuckled. "What'd he say?"

"That my heart was black and get the hell out of his house. Just for the record, I didn't 'fall away' from church. It fell away from me when the religious right took over. New Agers believe all dogmas go to heaven. I'll pass, thank you. I'll catch a wormhole to the next galaxy. I want to go to the same heaven dogs go."

"Did you watch any of the Pence-Franklin Graham debate?"

"Ohmygod, I never laughed so hard in my life. Just what we need, a Most Pious to lead the most pious prigs on the planet. Remember when the moderator asked them what color Jesus was? They both said '*White.*' Pence says it was part of the immaculate conception miracle. '*Jesus was the only white Jew in Jerusalem.*' What was another good part . . .oh yeah, when the moderator asked Pence who crucified Jesus and Pence says, '*Hillary. There's historical evidence of that in Revelations.*' Then Franklin says, '*I believe it was Two Corinthians, Mike, just like our Majesty said,*' and Pence shakes his head and looks like he's passing a stone. The best part—shit! Remember when Pence was asked if it was true he didn't like being alone with a woman who wasn't his wife? Franklin says, '*You stole that from my daddy. That's the Billy Graham Rule.*' '*At least I follow it,*' Pence says, and Franklin says, '*Oh yeah? Well everybody knows you eat Marie Callender's pies in your room,*' and Pence shoots back, '*That's better than eating Edwards,*' and Graham says, '*What's that supposed to mean?*' and Pence says, '*Nothing, you political hack.*' They had to cut away to a commercial."

They sat laughing. "Pharisee Franklin," Jason said. "How many mulligans are in Trump's harem, Frankie? He's nothing like his daddy. Did you know the Tombs are passing around collection plates for gold jewelry? They're making a golden image of Trump to replace the Lincoln Memorial."

"Are you kidding?"

"I heard it on the radio coming over here."

"Aren't you glad you're not one of them?"

"I'm the spawn of one of them. It's in my DNA. I'm an innocent victim of genetic stupidity."

"I read that DNA can be reprogramed."

"If you're a positive thinker or learn self-hypnosis. What's the point? While I'm lying there editing my cells, Trump will launch a bomb. I've gone over all this already with Amy."

"Argued, you mean."

"I don't argue, not since my father died. I discuss, I reason, I joke."

"But you're still angry. Mentally it grinds your guts."

Jason smirked. "Interesting skewed metaphor. I could sit here and talk till the cows turn blue."

"Why do you stay at your job? You hate it. You can get something better, with your background."

"I've been thinking about doing something online, earn easy money, jobs that really pay, be my own boss."

"Like what?"

"Customer service rep. Fake an accent so I have trouble understanding the questions, read random answers from a book, sell six more months of service when they try to cancel, tell them I'm transferring them to a supervisor, change my name to Derek and lower my voice a notch and play another round. Or accidently cut them off. Work in a cloud . . ." He stopped, listening. A vehicle with a large engine rumbled up the street. "What kind of truck is that at this hour?"

"I don't know."

"Could be a DACA bus. I heard this is how they're rounding up the illegals, sneaking up in the middle of the night. A big bus crawls in while everybody's asleep. The Bananas storm out like a container of rats scattering all over the neighborhood, pounding on doors, routing out families, little old people with walkers and oxygen tanks. The shouts and screams are horrible, all the neighbors wake up but they're too scared to do anything. A few try, though. The Bananas force them back, lob tear gas, armored vehicles roll in out of nowhere knocking over garbage cans. Some of it's been recorded for posterity. We don't even know if there's going to be a posterity. Maybe all we have now is a previous."

Phil stood and looked out the window. "It's gone. I think it was just the garbage truck."

"Maybe we're in posterity right now. We could be witnessing the pre-apocalyptic age. The Four Horsemen are in the starting gate, just waiting for the tweet."

"Do you need some coffee? I do." Phil began puttering in the kitchenette.

"What's behind door number three?" Jason asked.

"What?"

Jason nodded toward the door next to the bathroom.

"Not much. A sofa-bed. Computer. Mini-bar. Shower. Television. Enough in case I don't have time to go home."

"Did you ever think of getting a degree in psychotherapy, something like that, so you'd have decent hours? You wouldn't make more money, though."

"There are more important things than money."

"Easy for you to say. You're not selling Peeper Sleeper mattresses. I suppose it's too late for you to go back to college now, at your age."

"Thank you."

"How old are you?"

"As old as you think I am. How are you feeling?"

"Tired. Like my whole life flashed before my eyes in . . ." He glanced at his watch. " . . . in eighteen hours. You're not as fast as God. Did you hear about that prehistoric brain that was found pickled in a bog? It was an Iron Age man in his thirties, hanged and decapitated and his head fell in the bog and was preserved. That's how I feel right now. Like a pickled head."

Phil handed him a cup of instant coffee. "You know when your hypochondria started? The night your mother dropped the bombshell about your father's medical history. That scared the shit out of you."

"That doesn't mean I'm not a ticking bomb."

"You're not remembering to feel sick as often. And FYI, you haven't gripped your left arm since yesterday afternoon."

"I haven't had time."

"That's right."

"I have a sore throat. I don't feel happier about any of this."

"You're not going to feel happier yet, Jason, so get that out of your head. I never said you were going to feel happy when you left here. I said you would be a different man."

"Sadder but wiser, huh? Is that the payoff?"

"What payoff? Who gets a payoff?" Phil frowned and flipped a pencil into the air. It hit the desk, bounced and rolled off. "What have you seen since you've been here, Jason?"

Jason shrugged. "That this place is a shithole. That everything that scared me has happened. That it's worse than I thought it would be. That I'm really, really, really pissed and want to do something about it and I'm going to. Was Louie serious about me seeing this guy, Laszlo?"

"Absolutely."

"Wish I could remember where I heard that name. I'm going to look him up, though. I'm going to do it. I'm mad as hell and I'm not going to take it anymore, like that movie. I can actually feel my blood circulating. You know what that means? My body's quickening into action. More blood is flowing to my large muscles. This is important because I'll need the muscles in my arms and legs to fight off an attacker, or run if he's . . ."

Three sharp gunshots cracked the silence. Jason ducked and rolled over the arm of the chair and crouched in a tight ball on the floor, covering his head with both hands. Phil stood quickly and went aside the window, peering out. Herman's saxophone fell silent.

"Can you see them?" Jason whispered hoarsely. "How many are there? Are they looking up here?"

"No."

"No what? To which question?"

"To all three. Nobody's down there. The shots were close, though."

"How close? Stairway close? Hallway close?"

"Not in the building. Half a block."

Two more shots rang out, then several more.

"Get your gun! Get your gun!" Jason shrieked.

"I can't see who's shooting."

"So what? We won't get killed if we have a gun. That's the whole idea, isn't it? We need a spray of bullets from our side."

"I'm not shooting blind out the window."

"I'm not saying shoot blind. Maybe just walk past the window with your gun so they can see that you have one."

"Shut up, Jason." Phil made no move to retrieve his gun from the drawer.

"Oh Jesus, my alarm system's going off. I think my pupils are dilating. My saliva is definitely drying up. This is the worst place I've ever been in my life. If I'm dead before eight o'clock, I really think I'm due a partial refund."

"Sounds fair," Phil said. "Can I call you Rocko now?"

"Shut up yourself. You should have put foxholes up here."

The seconds ticked into interminable minutes. There were shouts, sounds of running. A vehicle roared by, walloping the air with heavy bass. A few more shots, but further down the way. Jason turned his head sideways on the hardwood floor. He could see Phil's feet standing close to the window. The floor was clean under the desk, no dust-balls, scraps of paper.

"Got any carrots in the fridge?" Jason asked.

"You're hungry for a carrot?"

"No. I need a weapon. Did you see that story about the girl who threw a baby carrot at a teacher as a joke? Hit the teacher in the forehead. The authorities said she might be charged with assault and battery. I never heard what happened."

"Was it a semi-soft carrot?"

"I don't know. I think it was a Dole midget."

"That's not politically correct anymore. They prefer to be called *little* Doles." Phil leaned forward to get a better look up and down the street.

"It's our God-given right to carry assault carrots," Jason said.

"If you have a concealed carrot permit."

"Gives a whole new meaning to packin' your lunch." Jason stretched his legs out on the floor, hands still locked over his head. "I always keep a bag of carrots in my refrigerator. Thank god I haven't had to use them yet."

"Would you know how?"

"Oh yeah. I was four when I held my first root. My father showed me how to use it. He wouldn't let me touch the big ones he kept locked in the vegetable bin. There was an old one he kept with a hair trigger. Called it his '*Big Woody*'" Jason was silent for several moments. "Those kids, the marchers, they were pulling it off. The NRA paid for Trump's coronation to try to shut that down. Do you think the kids are still organized?"

"Oh yeah. The way the adults botched everything?"

"Trumpinator: The Rise of the Teens. It's pretty quiet down there. Do you think somebody was shot?"

"Their friends will take care of them."

"I wonder if anybody took care of Gordon. I probably should have gone back."

"No. You needed to get out of there."

"If he'd been hit a lot worse, I could've called Santorum to give him CPR."

They heard the stairwell door to the street open and close. Someone began trudging slowly up the stairs, heavy-footed but steady, unlike someone wounded. Jason stopped breathing, listening, as the footsteps reached the landing, paused outside their door, then lumbered on up the next flight, then the next. Somewhere in the building, someone turned on a faucet, a water hammer vibrating the walls for several seconds. It stopped with a sudden loud thud.

Jason relaxed the iron grasp on his head "You know what veterans fighting in the Middle East call it over there? The suck. *'Embrace the suck.'* Do what you can. Do what you have to do."

"Not just over there anymore." They waited in silence several seconds. "Damn," Phil muttered.

"What? What's the matter?"

"It's too quiet down there."

"Hey Jason!" someone yelled from the street. "Come down here for a minute."

"Oh shit. *Shit*. Does he mean me?"

"Come on down, Jason. I know you're up there. We just want to talk to you a minute."

"That's Gordon Teasley. I knew I should've gotten him a Band-Aid."

Two gunshots were followed by a rapid succession of bullets into the air.

"What should I do?" Jason whispered shrilly.

"Don't go down there." Phil crawled to the front of his desk.

"Hey Ja-son. If you don't come down, we're coming up. We got you now, and your little car, too!" They whooped and laughed loudly. The downstairs door banged open and the sound of heavy boots clamored up the stairs.

"Get up!" Phil shouted. He shoved open the window. "Get up, Jason! You have to jump!" Jason scrambled to the window and climbed out onto the ledge.

"Try to land on the roof of your car. I'll give you a hard push. Don't try to drive. Just take off running toward that side-street Amy took. Go the way I told her."

Something heavy slammed the office door. On the second assault it began to splinter. With a powerful boost from Phil, Jason launched himself from the ledge.

As he hurtled through the darkness there was only one thought in Jason's terror-stricken mind. If he didn't make it out alive, would Amy wait for him?

—13—

Jason hit the floor hard, landing in a crouched position on his hands and knees. His heart pounded violently, and he gasped for air several seconds. Wherever he landed, it didn't feel like the roof of his car. Or concrete. The surface was smooth and dry. The place he was in was quiet. Compared to the murderous racket just moments ago, it was dead quiet.

Was that it? He was dead? Wasn't he supposed to go through a tunnel or something, see a bright light? Every cell in his body was trembling. He slowly opened his eyes. A lamp in the corner of the room was turned on; the smooth fabric of a sofa brushed his bare arm. He eased back on his haunches with growing disbelief.

This was his apartment. It was daylight. He looked around the room, then stopped and stared at an object on the wall next to the bookcase. It was a painting of a shipyard.

"Jesus!" he uttered. "Jesus." His face was cold with sweat. He put an elbow on the sofa and hoisted himself up. He stared again at the painting, waiting for his vital organs to stop quaking.

This whole thing was a nightmare? It couldn't have been. It was too real. Two minutes ago, Phil was shoving him out the window. He could still hear the door being bashed in. As he was falling through the darkness he knew there was no way he would land on his car. He knew he'd never make it out alive. In those fast-flying moments before his body hit pavement, his final thoughts were of Amy.

The adrenalin rush to his brain woke him just before he died, thank God. Although it might have been interesting to see what happened next. He couldn't wrap his head around any of it. It was too sudden a leap from REM sleep to reality. How much of the nightmare was true? Every day, every hour it seemed, breaking news exploded with another Trump atrocity. He snatched his cell phone from the coffee table and quickly tapped a number.

A woman answered. "Nine-one-one. What's the address of your emergency?"

"You're still there? Okay good. This isn't an emergency. I just have a question. Who's president of the United States?"

"Sir . . ."

"Yeah, I know this sounds like a prank but it's not, I swear."

"Donald Trump is president."

"Is that all?"

"Isn't that enough?"

"I mean, he's not emperor or anything, is he? He didn't crown himself, did he?."

"I'm transferring you to . . . ."

"No! Never mind. I'm sorry. I'm not awake. Sorry."

Was the breakup with Amy even true? Maybe she didn't leave him. Maybe that was part of the nightmare. He stumbled into the bedroom.

She was gone. Every trace of her. Her clothes, her shampoo, her toothpaste. She had even washed the sheets to remove her scent. He went to the kitchen and opened the refrigerator. Even the lard. Gone. She must have come back sometime after midnight when he was in deep sleep on the couch. He looked at his watch. He'd been out almost eighteen hours! REM only lasts maybe two hours before you cycle back to stage one. He must have had a transcendental experience. No wonder he had to pee.

When he came out of the bathroom he sat on the edge of the bed, rubbing his head. Everything was so confusing. He didn't know what was real. He had to talk to Amy. She was the only one he trusted to tell him the truth. What day was this? Wednesday, the day she usually rode the ferry to Bainbridge and back. She was probably taking the stairway right now from Pike Place down to the waterfront to catch the sunset crossing. If he hurried he could catch it.

It was late afternoon when he parked the Prius close to the Alaskan Way Viaduct. Left turns were still legal so he made quick time. He jogged to Colman Dock, Pier 52, spotting no orange sashes anywhere along the way. The Seattle Ferry terminal holding area for Bainbridge Island was packed with cars, trucks, campers and semi's in long numbered lanes, already being efficiently swallowed, Noah's Ark style, into "the boat," as locals called it. Dozens of people riding bikes and motorcycles were loaded first. The pedestrian bridge would be filled with rush hour foot traffic. It was the last ferry crossing before sunset.

About ten minutes before departure, Jason walked up a fairly steep ramp into the terminal. Still no orange sashes, no Bananas standing by the ticket counter inspecting wrists. He checked his own; it was clean. He purchased a ticket and stood off to the side of the waiting room until most of the foot traffic had boarded. He lifted the hood of his windbreaker over his head and walked quickly over the bridge onto the MV Wenatchee. He hadn't seen Amy but knew she was there, most likely on the top deck facing the open waters of Elliott Bay. The weather, although not perfect, wasn't cold or windy enough to force her inside. The boat held twenty-five hundred passengers, so it was unlikely she would spot him, but he kept a low profile anyway. He didn't want her storming off the boat before he had a chance to talk to her. He slid into a bench seat on the enclosed lower passenger deck and stared aft out the large window. He felt like a stalker. He checked his cell for messages. None from Amy, several from his boss, Huckleberry Harry.

The crossing to Bainbridge Island took about thirty minutes. When the engines rumbled to life, too late for her to jump ship, he stood and started toward the stairwell to the upper deck. What a laugh if Amy wasn't on board after all, after all this covert planning. His legs felt like rubber as he mounted the stairs. He walked out onto the sun deck and started to turn.

There she was, the collar of her blue rain parka turned up around her ears. A cold breeze blew off the frigid water beneath overcast skies. She stood alone, leaning against the rail, her hands deep in her pockets, watching a forty-foot schooner cutting northward under full sail. He walked over and stood beside her, careful not to touch her.

She started to turn his direction, recognized who it was and turned her head sharply toward the schooner's wake.

"I'm not here to argue with you about anything, Amy. I need you to answer some things for me. You're the only person I can trust."

"I don't know anything more than I knew yesterday."

"We had a big fight, right?"

"Wow," she half-laughed. "You weren't even paying attention to that."

"And you moved out."

"Yes. Please leave me alone now, Jason."

"I will. I promise. I just want to ask you a few things. I'm very confused. I had a bad dream, a very bad dream. I'm having trouble waking up from it. I just need you to tell me what's true and what isn't true."

She peered suspiciously at him. "All right."

"Donald Trump is president. He didn't crown himself emperor."

"No. He would if he could, though."

"Was Mueller fired?"

"Close. Not yet."

"Was California sold to pay for the wall?"

She snickered. "No. Good grief, Jason, what kind of dream did you have?"

"The nightmare kind. Did Russia hack into our computer grids? Power, nuclear, airline?"

"Yes. You said they were testing the systems to see if they could."

"And nobody's doing anything about it?"

"Not as far as I know."

"Is there any talk about Trump tattoos, proving our loyalty. Nobody can buy or sell anything unless we have one?"

"Not that I've heard." She looked worriedly at him. "I took your pulse last night when you were sleeping. You scared me. You looked dead."

"I might have sub-consciously fainted. The Bananas were after me."

"What?!"

"Is Trump putting his logo on all the bombs and missiles before his big parade?"

"No. Just the parade."

"Are the Complicits killing Medicare and Medicaid to pay for their tax booty?"

"They're talking more about it."

"Removing bank sanctions? I need to close my savings account."

"They did. You did already."

"Forty-seven dollars is a lot of money. I'm so grateful the billionaires let it trickle down to me. I'm starting to remember more, now. Clean air, clean water, clean meat, all kaput, right?"

"I don't think kaput yet. It's kind of hard keeping up with everything going on."

"The news is all fake except Fox, right?"

"That's funny you mention that. Last night before you got home I was watching the local news and the anchor read this thing, this warning about watching out for all the fake news out there, not to trust it. My dad this morning was so upset; he said the station is owned by Sinclair, a big news group that owns local news channels all over the country.

The anchors have to read exactly what the script says because they're under contract. He said it was written by a reporter for some Russian propaganda outlet, RT. Is it really happening, Jason? Are we being taken over?"

"They're working hard on it. Have you ever heard of a guy name Laszlo? Is it somebody we know?"

She thought a moment. "Wasn't he the good guy in Casablanca? He was something like a famous resistance fighter against the Nazi's."

"Did you tell me to go see a psyche detective named Phil Magnum?"

"No."

"You didn't say that if I didn't go see him, you were leaving me?"

"No. I said I couldn't take your complaining anymore. Then I left. When I came back you were sleeping on the couch. Who's Phil Magnum?"

"An undigested bit of beef, an underdone potato."

"Why does everything connect to a movie with you?"

"I don't know that movie, so I can't connect." Jason lapsed into silence, absently watching the Bainbridge Island shoreline. "I need to go to the Crosshairs District tomorrow."

"Why would you go there? It's dangerous."

"I need to see if a bird's there. And a man behind a green door."

She looked around helplessly. "You're scaring me, Jason. I'll go home with you, okay? We can watch TV until you're feeling better. I'll make some dinner."

"You can't."

"Why not?"

"You took the lard."

"Don't you have to work tomorrow?"

"No. I quit."

"You quit? When?"

"Just now."

-14-

The first thing he did upon awakening, after catching up on the news with two cups of coffee, was compose a simple, brief letter of resignation to Peeper's Sleepers Mattress Outlet, Attention: Harry Gumm, Manager.

Jason thanked them for his time in their employment, that he enjoyed being the best Sales Teammate in the company's history, that he was grateful he was able to substantially increase bottom-line company profits, get more prospects, close more sales, and consistently outsell their competition, and his last day would be two weeks from the current date. He printed it out, signed his name after Sincerely, then took a long, hot shower.

Harry Gumm was in the back-room office when Jason reported to work at five minutes to nine. He peered out the small window that looked into the showroom, spotted Jason, checked his watch and ambled out. He was wearing a new brown and gray argyle sweater-vest, and the usual frown.

"You're almost late," Harry barked. He followed Jason into the locker room.

"But I'm not." Jason punched his time card, smiled up at the surveillance camera as he always did, took off his jacket and removed a white envelope from an inside pocket.

"Truck's coming in this morning," Harry said. "You need to help unload it."

"Where's Colby?"

"He quit. You need to fill in till I hire somebody else."

"Two somebody-elses." Jason handed Harry the envelope.

Harry read the letter, his mouth slowly drooping open, his brows furrowing. "I don't understand this," he said.

"I'm sorry," Jason said. "Did I leave something out?"

"You're quitting?"

"Yes."

"After I hired your sorry ass after you were fired?"

"That's right. Yes." Two co-workers wandered over to a closer listening position.

"You can't quit. I'm firing you! It's going on your record, buddy. Nobody's going to touch you with a ten-foot pole!"

"I don't know, Harry. It depends on whose pole it is."

"That's it! You're fired, you faggot! Get out of here!"

"You're firing me because I'm gay? That's illegal in this state. Thank you, Harry. I need the money." Jason slipped his jacket back on. "Oh, before I forget, I have a present for you." He removed something from his pocket and held out a closed fist.

Harry hesitated, then extended his hand. Jason dropped two heavy steel one-inch marbles into his hand. "They're steelies. I've had them for years but I never needed them."

"What the hell am I supposed to do with these?"

"Keep them in your pants pocket, Harry. They'll give you something to play with, something to aspire to." He turned to leave, then paused. "By the way, do you know why dogs lick themselves? Because they can."

It was nine-thirty when he turned onto Twine Street, a seedy part of town known locally as the Crosshairs District. Except for the usual litter and a few homeless souls wandering aimlessly, the early morning streets were empty. Misdemeanors in this precinct usually didn't start until ten a.m., simple assaults from noon to nine, violent crime peaking around midnight.

Jason parked across from the Halyard-Winch building then just sat there, looking around. No yellow lines, no plaintive saxophone, no lone bird watching him, no writing on the second story window, just dirty glass. He checked his rearview mirror and wondered, for the second time in his life, what time miscreants and thugs and carjackers usually hit the streets, but this time he wasn't nervous. He felt a strange, almost invigorating peace.

Not far beyond the end of Twine Street, a double-decker trainload of freight clattered and rolled through Balmer Yard. Jason rolled down the window. He could smell the cold salt water and fish and tidal flats of the Sound. Nostalgic, home-grown comforting smells. He hadn't noticed them yesterday. The storefronts were about what he expected, except Spraytan Orange hadn't set up shop yet.

He got out, locking the door, and headed up the street looking for a green door. This was stupid, he knew this was stupid, but he felt compelled to do it anyway. Nothing about life made sense anymore.

Two blocks up he came to a small diner, Pete's Eats in old faded letters. Didn't look like a recent name change from the Acid Reflux. No BBB sign in the window. An old man was sweeping debris away from the front door.

"Do you have BBB by any chance?" Jason asked.

"What's that?" the man said.

"Bread and broth for a buck. You know, for the homeless."

"No, I don't know. And no, I don't." He went back to sweeping, thinking about it.

My god, there was the hotel, the HOT L with the missing E! Some local news station must have run a feature on it, a Seattle history segment. How else would he know about it?

He walked on, checking doors on both sides of the street for two more blocks, and then there it was. It was cracked and faded and almost obscure, but definitely a green door. It wasn't locked. A cluster of battle-weary mailboxes clung to a wall just inside the door, no names, just labels with letters—XL, BS, AI, FU. Jason smirked and started up, taking shallow breaths as he inspected the steps for spider webs. The place reeked of musty dust.

Jason hit the first landing and continued up the next flight. Louie said it was on the third floor, so fine, we're going to do exactly what imaginary Louis said. On the third floor he saw a green door at the end of the hall. He stood staring at it, then slowly approached it and stopped. This was some scary shit but compared to the nightmare . . ..He hesitated, then knocked once, a single decisive knock.

"Yeah?" A sleepy young guy with tousled hair opened the door.

"Are you Laszlo?"

"Who?"

"Laszlo. I don't have a first name."

"No. Wrong door." He started to close it.

220

"No, wait! Do you know anybody named Laszlo?"

"No. Sorry, bud. I gotta get back to work." He noticed Jason noticing his pajamas. "On my computer," he said.

Jason nodded. "Well, thanks anyway." He didn't move.

The young man took pity. "What does Laszlo look like? Maybe I've seen him coming or going."

"I don't know. All I have is the name."

"I've heard it before, someplace."

"Casablanca."

"Oh yeah. Kinda missed your time portal, didn't you?"

Jason smirked. "Funny."

"I'm a funny guy. Except today. And last night. And all day yesterday. You wouldn't have a punchline in your pocket by any chance."

"You're a comedian?" The guy frowned and shrugged. Jason said, "What's the line?"

"Something like, 'Trump's a lousy businessman. How many times has he filed bankruptcy?' I lose it here. Nothing's coming to me."

Jason mulled it over a few seconds. 'No wonder Trump files bankruptcy so often. He has a one-night stand and it cost him a hundred and thirty thousand dollars.'"

"Yeah! Is that yours? Can I buy it from you?"

"That's okay. My contribution to the war effort."

"Getting bananas for real, isn't it? Mueller subpoenaed my WTF list. Trump's screwing to be a dictator."

"Making us *great* all right, a bunch of Bananas marching down Ivanka Avenue."

"I'd love to deflate that bloviating asshole."

"Before he crowns himself emperor. He's lining up all his key players."

"The emperor with no clothes."

"Can't trust those Russian laundries."

"Not completely their fault. The seams on his profiteering keep splitting out."

"Blubber orange. Not just his face anymore."

"Maybe Spanky likes parading naked."

"He's golfed a lot of holes."

The young man smirked. "Man, I wish some of my friends at the club were here. They'd love to roast that prick. We should organize." He thought a moment. "You . . . do you want to come in for a minute? I just made some coffee."

"Yeah. Thanks. My name's Jason."

"I'm Louie."

Jason stopped. "Are you kidding me?"

"Not intentionally. Is Louie a funny name?"

"No. It's just that, you know, Louie and Rick walking into the fog and Bogart says . . ." He was so close to saying it. "Never mind."

Jason followed him inside. "Trump's like the shark in Jaws," he said. "The Great White eating machine. The politicians cover for him for the money."

"We're going to need stronger punchlines," Louis said.

Jason closed the door behind him. "We're going to need a bigger boat."